ABOUT THE AUTHOR

Werner J. Egli's novels are published in German-speaking Europe, where he received some of the most prestigious awards for his writing. For TUNNEL KIDS he was nominated for the *Hans Christian Andersen-Medal.* His books have been translated into a variety of other languages. Werner lives with his family near Zurich, Switzerland, and in Tucson, Arizona.

Blues for Lilly

A young man's search
for his past and his future

A NOVEL BY

Werner J. Egli

Published by ARAVAIPA-Verlag
Zelgmatt 24, CH-8132 EGG bei Zürich, Switzerland
First published in Germany by C. Bertelsmann/Random House, Munich,2001
Copyright by Werner J. Egli, 2018
All rights reserved
ISBN: 978-3-03864-409-5
Jacket design: flin
Shutterstock: Daniel Ridge
Translation: James Pierce
Edited by Esther Porter
Realisation: Brigitta Vasella

Acknowlegments

Bergie Harzheim proofread the first draft of the translation. Thanks, Bergie! It would not have happened without your tremendous help, and without Esther Porter, my editor, and her fine-tuning the final draft.

For Jim

It was the wish of my American translator James Pierce to get this book done befor he died.

Rest in Peace, my friend.

CHAPTER 1
A BEAUTIFUL DAY

What remains of Lilly, to this day, is the gift she gave me when I looked into her eyes for the last time. It's perhaps the most valuable treasure that I had yet to discover. One has to imagine it: a human is dying, and in the eyes is such a pleasant glow, such radiance, that Death himself could have warmed his hands near it. To be there with her, sharing her last hours, the legacy Lilly left for me was hidden in that glow. It wasn't gold or jewels, nor was it a fortune in some secret bank account. And, despite that, I sensed Lilly couldn't have given me anything more valuable; nothing could have made me richer. I still cannot explain it adequately. Maybe that's why I'm writing this book. So I will be able to retrace every inch of the way we walked together, relive every minute we spent together, and learn to comprehend what I discovered the day Lilly left me behind, mourning — but with joy at the same time. Love it was, pure and simple. Today, I know it. But, at the time, I thought that for someone like me, there was nothing left to discover. I had experienced everything — was firmly convinced I had lived through it all.

As Hanna's father, George Ledbetter, put it to my mother, I had an unusual, natural gift.

"With Bradley, you won't know what's hit you," he had warned her. "Maybe it's a gift, but it could also be a curse."

"With all due respect, Mr. Ledbetter, I don't believe I

quite understand. Would you care to explain what you mean?" my mother had asked him.

"Bradley manages to make people talk, without it being his intention. He only has to enter a room, and that's enough to make people tell him about their lives. My wife told him how we lost a set of twins before they were born. She's never talked about it to anyone, but she believed she could share her sorrow with Bradley. When I happened to come into the room, she was crying."

"And why should this be a curse? It's probably true that there few people with whom one would want to share one's mourning."

"Indeed," Mr. Ledbetter agreed.

My mother didn't know what he had meant by this, but when she told me about the conversation later, I could make quite a good guess. Maybe he meant that, at some point, I would go crazy if I continued to burden myself with the problems of others. Apart from that, of course, he didn't want me to use this unique, natural gift to ruin Hanna's life, for which he already had a plan — for her own good; that goes without saying.

Of course, he had no clue how much I could handle without going crazy. You see, I was tough, despite my young age. After all, I had already lived through a great deal. I had already lost people who meant a lot to me. My father, for example, after he more or less stole Alesha from me and destroyed a dream. And McDelcott, my mother's husband, who could never be a father to me no matter how often he tried. At least for my brother, Mitch, he represented specific support for a while. I was too old to bother with such comforts. I had experienced a feeling that I took for love, and for the first time when I was overwhelmed by my desire, I made a complete fool of myself. I had carried my heart around as if I wanted to sacrifice it to some god, and it shattered in my hands. I had licked my wounds when they were still bleeding until only a bitter taste was left. During that trying time, I also lost my friend Santiago Gomez. In the cold gray of dawn, when he got killed by a bullet from a border patrol agent, anger made me come across my own shadow, which warned me about myself. "I'm not only your shadow," it had said. "Try not to lose me."

Yes, I had felt the pain of loss. But what I saw in Lilly's eyes the day we said goodbye, that glowing fire of love. I must have looked for it because I guessed that there must be a love different from what I felt when I was sitting with Hanna down at the Brewster Pond. And I became aware of how much I missed Alesha and the fact that I preferred to go into town and look for her. I couldn't be with anyone without thinking of her, not even with Hanna.

I had believed I already knew everything. One night, I chose not to sleep down by the riverbank under open skies. Instead, like the man I wanted to become, I secretly went to Alesha. I was still a boy when I drove to Dickens without a driver's license, went to her motel room and knocked on the door. She opened it, and behind her, a pink light was shimmering, which almost made me dizzy. She didn't say a word but only looked at me. She didn't say, "Why did you come here?" because she knew why.

She was wearing a thin, almost transparent nightdress, and I stood in front of her without knowing what to do. Then she took me by the hand and pulled me inside and embraced me; we kissed, and I pulled her against me. And somehow, to this day, I don't know how exactly it all happened, but what seemed like the next minute, we were lying on the bed. Since that time, that moment in a motel room where I became a man, I believed I could say that I knew everything about love.

Only today do I understand that it wasn't until I looked into Lilly's eyes that I encountered true love. I know that now, after three years have gone by. Three long years that made me a man.

I sometimes dream that, when my time comes, I'll die just as happy as Lilly. She was happy to have lived. Happy to have taken the path she had been looking forward to for months, just like leaving for a nice long trip to a far-away country. And sometimes, I still wish, not only when I'm dreaming, that I had been able to accompany her to the place from which, thank God, there is no turning back. Where, one day, Alesha will go too.

Lilly went alone. She had looked at only me before she closed her eyes forever as if I were the hero who had led her through the dark. After she'd got lost in a labyrinth, she finally realized she hadn't been wandering in alone.

I was only still a teen, and all the roads I knew led through my screwed-up world to nowhere.

Yes, I wanted to be with her when she died, alone with her in those precious moments. That was my greatest wish at the time, and I was lucky that it got granted. So

I took her by the hand as if I knew the way, and I cried, even though I was happy with her - for her - happy as never before.

It was a day full of mysteries and miracles. We had eaten together, just the two of us, but with all the others in the large dining hall with the many tables and the windowed front that faced the garden. I had brought a candle, and on the table, in the flickering light, there was a photograph of JB in a silver frame. We had turkey in cream sauce, little potato fritters, and spinach with grated cheese. Lilly took two or three gulps from a glass of red wine and dabbed her lips with her napkin. She made every hand movement carefully and attentively as if she were worried this dinner wouldn't remain in her memory.

Lilly no longer ate much, but everything she did eat, she savored, almost as if she believed this meal to be her last. She wanted caramel pudding for dessert, of which she ate two small spoonfuls.

"Now, that will do," she said after that. "Come on, Brad, let's go."

I helped her to her feet, supporting her by holding her arm, the way I'd done hundreds of times before. We walked slowly between the tables, and the others watched us with wide eyes, curious where we would go, though there was only one door, which led to the long hallway, as they all knew well. And some of them said "Goodnight, Lilly," or, "We'll see each other in the garden." Lilly only smiled, and the smile was her goodbye, without anyone realizing it or having a chance to be sad.

We took a stroll together through the small garden, and she held onto my arm. Sometimes we stopped so she could look at the flowers and the grass. She touched the leaves of an ornamental shrub with her free hand, as if, in them, she sensed the pulse of eternal life. Nothing seemed to escape her, but she didn't stop to talk to anyone. She didn't appear to notice the people sitting on the benches in the evening sun, looking at us as if we were two odd strangers who had gotten lost. And then, when the sun was setting, sinking into the crowns of the old trees, making their green glimmer, it became cold and we went upstairs to her room. There was her large bed and the TV and the chest and the commode with the tilting mirror and the photos and the rose, which had dried a long time ago and was only still blooming in Lilly's memory.

I placed JB's photo in the silver frame next to the others and opened the window to let in air and light, but by then, the sun had gone down somewhere beyond the Mississippi. The evening sky colored the walls of her room a dark red, and if I had remained by the window, I would have seen the Mississippi through the trees. The grand old man, as Lilly often called this mighty river respectfully, only bright patches of moving water, which, from here, I could imagine more than I could see. And I would have heard the town, the subdued, steady noise that was everywhere and nowhere, and maybe whispering voices coming up from the garden, where old people were sitting on benches.

I sat on the chair next to Lilly's, picked up JB's guitar

and played it softly. I played nothing special, nothing she hadn't already heard before. I was picking the strings quietly; smiling at her while tears ran down my cheeks, her hands lying motionless on the white bed cover. The wrinkles in her face smoothed themselves, and her bright eyes were gleaming. I admired her one more time, praised her for her delicateness and the strength hidden inside her. I admired her for her beauty and her zest for life, which often allayed my fear of an uncertain future.

Of course, I knew who she was thinking of the moment she closed her eyes forever, reclining in a bed that never before seemed as large to me as it did right now.

The old guitar in my hands had a voice only Lilly could hear. No matter what tune I played, it was JB playing. I no longer existed for my beloved Lilly. I was no longer present.

She died while I played. She didn't need to say goodbye. She had already done that when we came into the room. She had changed in the bathroom, had groomed herself, combed her hair one last time, and washed. And when she lay down on the bed, and I pushed the pillows behind her back and head, she kissed me.

"It was a good life, Brad," she said. "I couldn't expect as much as I got. Yes, I was very fortunate."

"You are still alive," I answered, smiling. I smiled to hide my fear of losing Lilly, but the smile and the fear gradually disappeared like shadows at dawn.

My dear Lilly. I knew she was dead now, though she looked as if she were asleep. I knew this face. With this smile, she wanted to tell me one last time how much she was looking forward to everything that came after death. On a path, no wheel had ever rolled. A soft tune in the wind coming from somewhere never a shot was fired. A glistening sky, as she remembered it from her youth when she still believed summer would last forever. No walls. No bars. Not even a threatening thundercloud is pushing itself across the horizon. And somewhere, anywhere in this never-ending landscape, he would be waiting for her. She would run to him, light-footed and carried by happiness, blonde hair flowing in the wind, a delicate dress. He would open his arms wide and pull her toward him with his strong hands, the way he hadn't dared to when they were both young.

I put JB's guitar on the chair and bent over her and kissed her forehead.

And I kissed her cheeks and took her hands in my hands and held them softly in fear they would turn to dust. The skin on her face was pale and soft, and I kissed her lips. And when I thought I felt her breath soft against my cheek, I froze, held my breath, looking with all my senses for one last touch, one last sigh; a breath.

The tears dried on my skin, and after a while, I took the pillows from behind her back. I left only the pillow behind her head. Then, I lay down next to her on the bed and folded my arms behind my head. I looked out the window, beyond the leaves of an old, gnarled oak, into the evening sky, crisscrossed with the vapor trails of jets. And only now did I notice the voices from the garden, soft voices of people who still had a stretch of life left, voices that carried on as if there was nothing wrong in the world — minds remaining unaware as Lilly died in her room so peacefully that no one, apart from me, had noticed.

I lay next to her for a long time, and I didn't notice the darkness setting in as the air grew cold. In my thoughts, I was with her, accompanying her on her path over meadows and through forests. It was autumn, and the weather was beautiful, everything was colorful and smelled of warmth, and then I saw JB sitting in front of his small house that had burned down years ago. He was in a dark suit and a white shirt, and there was a dark red rose in the buttonhole of his jacket. He laughed as she ran toward him, getting up from his chair. He started down the steps of the porch, a tall, gangly young man, with the sun shining on his face. He opened his arms.

"Lilly," he shouted as if he had been waiting for a long time. "Lilly, do you know how much I love you."

Yes, she knew it, and she never in her life had run as fast as she did now.

CHAPTER 2
A TALK WITH JIM FLETCHER

I took the elevator down. The air inside was terrible. It smelled of stale food and floor cleaner. In the beginning, when I visited for the first time, I was disgusted by the smell. I couldn't eat or drink anything there. I thought I would choke. At first, I didn't want to stay, not even for five minutes. Since then, I became so used to it that I wouldn't have preferred to be anywhere else.

Downstairs, I walked down the long corridor, which had pictures on the walls, painted by a classroom of children. Sunrises. Sunsets. Moons and stars. Hills with strange figures that looked like fish or antennae. Or airplanes.

A cage with a myna bird locked inside stood in a niche between the two windows. It liked to talk. One only had to walk by, and it would talk. Sometimes I stopped to listen. Today, I wasn't listening up to it. It said the same thing all the time anyway. "Feel like having some caviar?" No idea who had taught it that. "Feel like caviar?" and "What do you want? An old hat to drum on?"

A caregiver named Rhonda came from the kitchen through the steel swinging door, saw me walking by the cage, and smiled.

"Lilly hasn't eaten much," she said. "I noticed it when I cleaned the tables."

"Yes," I said. I couldn't think of anything else to say, and later, I couldn't explain to myself why I hadn't told Rhonda that Lilly had died. Perhaps, I just wasn't ready to say it out loud.

I walked outside and down the street, and my mother was sitting at McDonald's by the window, in the same seat where Lilly always sat when we went out for lunch. She was reading a celebrity magazine. Her French fries had gone cold and lay limply on the tray, most of them drenched in ketchup. She was drinking Dr. Pepper. I didn't know any other woman who liked Dr. Pepper. At home, our fridge was full of Dr. Pepper. She said Coke eats away at your stomach. She looked up when I came in, and she immediately could tell that Lilly was dead.

"Come here," she said and held out a hand toward me.

"It's all right," I said. I couldn't look at her.

I just kept standing there, staring out the window into the street. Outside, a humungous Ronald McDonald was waving to children, enticing them to come inside.

Alesha was somewhere out there in town. If I had known where I could find her, I probably would have gone to her. Just like that. I would have knocked at her door and said, "Here I am, and I want to stay with you."

"Brad, sit down next to me," my mom said, while she closed the magazine and shoved it into her bag. I kept standing and stared through the big window. "Brad! Come here and sit down with me!"

I shook my head without looking at her.

"Somebody needs to tell them she's dead," I said.

"You mean you haven't told anybody?"

"No. Now that Lilly's dead, you can tell them."

My mom got up from the bench and came to me. "Had you mentioned to her that I'm here?"

"No. Lilly didn't ask about anybody."

I looked her straight in the eyes, and she didn't avoid eye contact. She was good at standing up to my gaze. I had always been the first to look away. Not this time. All I felt were tears that I wanted to shed. I remembered the day JB had told me that the art of life consisted of hiding one's pain behind a smile. But at that instant, I didn't succeed in doing so.

"Then I'll go now and tell them," she said. "Are you going to stay here?"

I nodded, and she left. I ordered a Coke and thought I should call Hanna to tell her we would stay in Memphis for a few days and that we probably wouldn't be back in Winstel before Saturday, as all the formalities had to be dealt with first.

I walked to the phone with the Coke in my hand and called Hanna. Her father picked up.

"Ledbetter." That's all he said, but somehow, it always sounded like a warning. For a moment, I thought about hanging up, but then I asked to speak to Hanna. This time, I didn't change my voice as I'd often done when I didn't feel like talking to him.

"Is that you, Brad?" he asked. "I thought you went to Memphis with your mother, to see Lilly."

"I am in Memphis, sir," I said.

"Ahh." He seemed to have to think for a second what to say to me next. And then, it came. Cold and hard, as if he had stored the words in a freezer, just waiting for the right time to use them on me.

"By the way, Brad, I must talk to you sometime soon

about certain things that are important to all of us."

Of course, I knew what he meant, but I played dumb.

"Things, sir? What things?"

"Well, Hanna's future, for example. And yours too, of course. You are a gifted young boy with great talent. That is why it's important to set goals. I assume you've set goals for yourself, haven't you, Brad?"

Of all the times to do so, he tried to put me on the spot now. Lilly hadn't even been dead for half an hour, and he was talking to me about my future. He didn't have the faintest idea. He was a clerk at our local bank, damn it, and one day they had elected him mayor of Winstel because nobody else wanted the job. I would have loved to tell him to get lost, but I didn't have the strength at the time.

"Yes, sir, when I'm back..."

"But indeed, Brad. Hang on. Hanna's just coming in." I heard him call for her. His voice sounded muffled. Most likely, he was holding his hand over the receiver, but I could still hear him. "Call for you, Hanna." And then Hanna's voice came on from afar, probably from the front door, through the corridor, and into the living room. "Who is it? Brad?" Then Mr. Ledbetter again, "Who else?" Some noises followed, and I imagined Hanna throwing her sports bag onto the floor and tearing the receiver from her father's hand before he could say goodbye to me.

"Brad! Is it you?"

"Yes."

"You... sound so close... as if you were here in

Winstel."

"I'm in Memphis. I just wanted to tell you that we probably won't be back before Saturday, my mom and I."

Seconds went by. I could hear her breathing. Somewhere, a door got shut.

"Nice of you to call me," she said. "I had hoped you would call me."

"I just wanted to tell you that we won't..."

"Today is only Tuesday," she interrupted. "Thursday you want —"

She broke off because all of a sudden she understood and was probably holding her breath.

"Brad, she is... Oh, my God, she's died, hasn't she?"

"Yes."

"Oh, poor Brad," she sobbed. "Dear God, I'm sorry for you. I know how much you cared for her. And now she's gone. I cannot believe it. It's terrible. So unfair, especially as you've so much looked forward to seeing her again and now. Oh, Brad, if I only knew what to say. I wish I could comfort you. It's all so sad; I think I'll start crying."

"Hanna, it's..."

She started crying, and there was nothing I could have done for her. So I said goodbye and hung up. I walked back to the table and sat down by the window and looked out at the street, watching cars turn into the McDrive, mothers with happy children. And for some reason, I thought, man, if some nut suddenly came into McDonald's and started to shoot right now, just shooting at everything that moved, at the mothers and the children and the employees and the old man sitting bent over at one of the small tables putting away a cheeseburger... Imagining made me feel sick. I took a good look at the next driver turning in and saw that he was wearing overalls and a dirty baseball cap with a Texaco star on it. I told myself that he was an ordinary car mechanic, who had a wife and three or four kids at home. The next car was a patrol car with two cops inside. They parked and came in, and they both ordered strawberry milkshakes. I took a good look at them. One was quite a bit older than the other, his mustache had already turned gray, and the younger one was black, wearing aviator sunglasses. I wondered whether I should ask if they knew Alesha and where she lived. But I didn't because there was probably no point in asking about a girl in a city of a million people when I only remembered her first name. Elvis had already tried that in a Chuck Berry song Mom listened to on the old record player when she was thinking about happier times.

The cops left and got back into the patrol car. They sat and drank their milkshakes, and they probably had their radio on and were just hoping that somewhere, something would happen and that their operator would give them orders to go into action.

Then Mom came back. She was worn out. I could tell, even though she made an effort not to let on. She must have cried. There was something smudged on her left eye, probably eyeliner.

She bent down and hugged me.

"You were with her when she died, weren't you?" she

said.

I nodded.

She got up. "Did she say anything before she died?"

I nodded again.

"About your father, I mean."

"No."

"I tried to call him. He should at least know his mother died. He wasn't home." Mom ordered another Dr. Pepper and came back with the plastic cup. She sat down in the same place she had sat before.

"Perhaps you should call him later, Brad."

"Me?"

"He's your father, right? We'll bury Lilly's urn with her ashes at home in Winstel. Tell him that. Tell him that he could at least come to the funeral. That's the least, I think."

"We will take Lilly's ashes down to the Mississippi and spread them over the water, Mom. That was her wish."

My mother looked at me. "Did she tell you that's what she wanted?"

"Yes. When JB died, she told me. Lilly spread JB's ashes over the Mississippi. From the middle of the Mississippi Bridge, that's where I'll spread Lilly's ashes."

"Are you sure it is not against the law to that. Spread ashes of dead people where ever you want too."

"I'm not going to ask anybody!"

"Then tell him that, Brad. Tell your father we'll spread Lilly's ashes over the Mississippi. He should at least know what you're planning. She's his mother, after all."

Of course, she was right. And that's just what I told

my father that evening on the hotel phone.

"Jim Fletcher," he answered.

"Brad," I said.

"Brad, damn, Brad! Where in hell are you, kid? Damn, we haven't seen each other for a long time. What's new? Where are you?" He laughed. "In trouble, aren't you? And now your father should help you to get out and…"

"Lilly is dead," I interrupted him.

He fell silent. A minute or more went by before he spoke again. "Brad, where are you?" His voice trembled.

"In Memphis."

"Have you been with the old lady when she died?"

"Yes."

"And who else? Your mother?"

"No. Mom is here, but I was alone with Lilly."

He was silent again.

"Hello?" I said. "Are you still there?"

"Of course, I'm still here. I've just been thinking about what to say to you."

"You don't need to say anything to me."

"Okay. Then I prefer not to say anything. What's going to happen now? I mean, there will probably be some kind of funeral. What did my brother, Lewis, say about that? Does he even know she died?"

"Mom says you should call him."

"I'll do that, Brad, no problem. When — when did she die?"

"Tonight. Just before seven o'clock."

"Just before seven?"

"Yes."

"I was still on the road then. You know that I'm driving trucks again, right? I was on my way home. Is your mom nearby?"

"Yes."

"Let me talk to her."

"She doesn't want to."

"Okay. Then tell me what I should do. When's the funeral, and where? Of course, I'll come to that. And Lewis too, I guess. I'll tell him."

"There won't be a funeral. She'll be cremated."

"Cremated? I'll be damned, Bradley. Why in hell would she do a thing like that for?"

"You should have asked her when she was alive. She told me to scatter her ashes over the Mississippi."

"Hmm, that's not a bad idea. I mean, what's left then, when one is cremated — "

"Ashes."

"Right. A little pile of rubble and ashes."

"And memories."

"Right." He seemed to be mulling over something. "What are your plans, Brad?"

"What do you mean?"

"Well, with the ashes. When's it going to happen?"

"No idea. Mom says that the cremation can take place the day after tomorrow. After that, we get the urn with the ashes, and since we're here in Memphis, we could scatter them over the river right away."

"Of course. It's probably better too, for Lilly, I mean, and for everybody else also. At least Lilly's in a better place now."

"Yes." I didn't know what to say. In a way, I did know but didn't say it.

"Hey, I'm damn glad that you were with her, Brad. Damn glad. I'll never forget."

"Okay."

"How are you then?"

"Okay."

"Okay?"

"Okay."

"Did you happen to hear from Alesha?"

I should have been prepared for that, but I wasn't. And so the blood shot to my head. My Mom, who was keeping a close eye on me, knew right away what was going on.

"Tell your father that the little slut left the county in the dead of night before they could stone her."

"Was that your mother?"

"Yes."

"What did she say?"

"She asked whether you're coming," I lied.

"To Memphis?"

"Yes. The day after tomorrow. You can do it."

"No. I can't. My job..." he cut off, seemed to think about some excuse. "Listen, Brad. You know me. I don't say I can come and then not show up. And I don't say I can't come and quickly think up some excuse. That's why I'm telling you I'm coming if you bring her to Winstel."

"Who?"

"Lilly."

"Lilly?" I thought his brain started to go bad on him.

"The ashes, damn it. Take the urn…"

"Don't let you be taken in by some kind of a horse trade," Mom said so loudly I got distracted. "You know what he's like. He'll chew your ear off when it's all about getting his…"

"Your mother keeps interrupting. Tell her to shut up for once."

"Mom, cut it out!"

"You take the ashes to Winstel, and I'll do my job here. As soon as I have the cash, I'll come down, and we can drive to Memphis together. You and me. What do you think? I believe Lilly would appreciate that."

"And how long until you have the cash? Two, three years, or what?"

"A few weeks, at the most. I happen to have started this new job. I told you I'm driving trucks again."

"Cross country?"

"Short distances for the time being. But later, I'm getting a cross-country route. Up north. New York to Seattle. That's why I can't leave right now. Probation, you understand. If I take off for a few days now, I lose the job, even if they say it's all right, this being about my mother's death and all."

"Okay," I said. "Then I'll take Lilly back to Winstel."

"Brad, listen. I'll never forget this. Say hello to your mother. And give me a holler when you're in Winstel. Or I'll call you. Okay?"

"Okay."

"Then — "

"Yes."

"We'll see each other."

"Yes."

It took a while before he hung up. I knew he loved me, but he was not able to tell me. My mother opened her magazine, a picture of Madonna on the front page. She rarely talked about herself. She was too busy making up a life for herself, and in the meantime, she had lost all sense of reality. Hers was a star-spangled life. When Johnny Depp got highlights in his hair — that was her life. And when Madonna came out with some crap about child education — that was her life too. And the Kennedys, of course. All the bad luck they had to endure. And Elvis was alive and was spotted somewhere or another all the time.

We'd never been a family. And we weren't a family the day Lilly died. We had only come to Memphis because I wanted to see Lilly one more time. And Mom, most likely, accompanied me because she was afraid I would see Alesha again and possibly run off with her. That's why she was with me. So that I didn't all of a sudden go crazy, the way my father once did when he left us. Only on rare occasions did he reappear, when he had nowhere else to stay.

That's why she was here with me in this hotel room, reading the exclusive interview with Tom Cruise.

"What have you worked out with him?" she asked without looking up.

"He wants to come."

She raised her head and looked at me. Her eyes became hard and sad at the same time.

"Here?"

"No. I'm supposed to take the urn to Winstel. Then he'll come, and we'll take the Greyhound bus to Memphis and scatter the ashes."

"He and you?"

"Yes."

She laughed out loud. "Brad, you know that you'll be waiting forever."

"He's promised he'll come to Winstel."

"Forever, Brad," she repeated.

"Ashes won't go bad," I said.

She looked at me as if I went bonkers — at her wit's end, yet somehow full of sympathy. I hated it when she looked at me like that. I still hate it today, even though she didn't look at me like that anymore since Mr. Blanchard, my English teacher, told her that I would probably go my way and become a writer. I'm her son, damn it. She and he, my father, created me. If I'm off the mark, what does that say about her? About her own life and mine and that of Mitch? If I'm off the mark, then they really should take a close look in the mirror, both of them.

"Ashes don't need to be kept in the fridge," I tried to explain to her. "He can come whenever he wants to."

I think she understood that. In any case, she shrugged her shoulders and continued reading. She just didn't like to talk about him. When she felt like it, she could talk a lot about Elvis. But she never felt like talking about my father. And I couldn't blame her for that, after what had happened with Alesha.

So we drove back home after the cremation, and

I got there one day earlier than I had told Hanna on the phone. I didn't call her. Of course, I knew that this would cause trouble, but I didn't care. I went home and called Wayne, my best friend, and told him that I was back and that I had brought Lilly's ashes. He wanted to see them, and so he came, and I opened the urn so that he could have a look. I mean Wayne wasn't one of those people who never thought about life and death. On the contrary, once when we were sitting together on the water tower, he told me that he couldn't sleep anymore because he woke up in the middle of the night. He was unable to stop thinking about what it would be like to leave this world and all the things that would stay behind, even though one would like to take them along. At the time, he thought it would be best, in the end, to be able to look back on a mediocre life, because then it would probably be easier to go.

I had no idea how Wayne came up with things like that. Most likely, he has a real chance to become very old. His grandparents were still alive, and he even had a living great-grandfather, who is being taken care of somewhere in Kansas, in an old people's home for Alzheimer's patients. That's because he cannot remember anything, except when one puts him in the sun. Honestly, Wayne's grandmother, who is over seventy years old herself, but still very fit, like her daughter, Wayne's mom, who is forty, told me this.

I know it's true, the part about the sun, I mean. It was just the same with Lilly. Every time we were sitting together in the garden, in the sunshine, a mysterious change would come over her; as if the sun was able to recharge her, with nothing but its light and its warmth.

It's much more blatant with Wayne's great-grandfather, though.

"When I get there, he doesn't recognize me," Wayne told me. "But then I wheel him out of his room, and we go out in the sun, and you'd think, I don't believe it, but it's as true as the fact that I'm squatting here next to you telling you this story. When he's in the sun for a while, he opens his eyes in a different way, and it's as if, up there in his head, the clouds start to lift. He recognizes me and even says my name, and then, when I take him back to his room, he's already forgotten everything. One should always leave him standing in the sun, but that's not possible I believe because it sometimes rains in Kansas."

That's how it is with Wayne's great-grandfather. Fortunately, Lilly never got Alzheimer's. She just loved to be sitting in the sun in the garden. She was always able to remember everything, even things that seemed unimportant. But I learned to pay attention to her words; I absorbed them like a sponge until I was able to write them down at home.

When Lilly, in her memories, found what she was looking for, she talked about JB most of the time. About love, the only true love of her life. And about the one big misfortune, through which her love was made eternal.

CHAPTER 3
WORN OUT SHOES

I was a skinny kid back then when I visited Lilly for the first time. I went with my father, who had been released from prison in Oregon a few days earlier. Out of the blue, he called me and said: "Kid, I'm coming by today, and then we'll go and visit grandma."

My grandma? I first had to mull over who that was. My grandmother. His mother. Jesus, I hadn't thought about her for such a long time she'd almost vanished from my memory.

He did come that day; he picked me up, and then we drove to Memphis together, accompanied by a blonde, whose name I can't recall. All I remember are her big tits, her cherry red lips and her high heel shoes she took off and tossed, one by one, over the backrest of the front seat right into my laps. They matched well, my father and her, my father wearing these dark shades, his hair styled and combed back with thick glossy mousse and the white shirt that looked way to large on him hanging loosely over his slacks. The coolest things I noticed about him were these blue suede shoes. The guy who wrote this famous song must have had a picture of my father, Jim Fletcher, in his head, my father wearing these fancy shoes back when we drove from Texas to Tennessee in that old convertible, Blondie next to my father, choppy air under her skirt and a colorful scarf wrapped tightly around her head to keep her hair in place, and me on that back seat, with hot, whirling wind in my curls and her shiny pumps in my lap.

Bits and pieces of Country Music out of the car radio flapping around my ears, a glance from father's eye in the rearview mirror and Blondies shiny white feet with the blood-red painted toenails on the dashboard.

It took us two days to get to Memphis, staying at a motel for one night. I had to sleep on a couch in a room for three with Jesus Christ hanging on the wall above me and a rattling air conditioner going full blast. I heard them laugh and giggle under a quilted bedspread thinking I was asleep, and after they were done I watched her naked in the moonlight tiptoeing to the bathroom while my father sat on the bed smoking a cigarette.

Once we arrived in Memphis, my father sent her off for a stroll and drove his old Chevy convertible up to the retirement home. He asked the lady at the reception for Lilly, and she asked him who she should say was here, but he didn't even tell her his full name or that he was Lilly's son. Instead, he only answered, "Tell Lilly Jim's here."

We waited downstairs, and the myna bird was there already and asked my father whether he fancied caviar, and my father tried to teach him in a low voice to say "bullshit." Meanwhile, I was watching three old men and one woman sitting at a round table and observing each other suspiciously, all four of them with a cup of coffee and a piece of cake in front of them on the table. I still remember how the one sitting in a wheelchair was slowly falling asleep, and how another, who was sitting directly opposite him, stole a piece of his cake. I couldn't believe my eyes. In those days, I still had an intact sense of justice. I drew my father's attention to what was going on at the table. My father said I should wake the old geezer up if it were so damn important to me. I didn't dare because one of them kept farting, but then the one in the wheelchair woke up, and of course, noticed that a piece of his cake was missing. He accused the wrong one of stealing it. The woman screamed that she couldn't take it any longer, this nagging about a stupid piece of cake. A nurse asked them to be quiet, and they went silent immediately, perhaps because otherwise the nurse would have kicked their shins. The myna bird then cawed "cool-tit" instead of "bullshit." I almost fell off my chair seconds later when the man in the wheelchair stole a piece of cake from the farter to his left, because he had fallen asleep, despite his farting.

I would have preferred to have run outside and strolled through the town with the blonde, but then Lilly appeared, petite and delicate, and I still remember that she only had a few strands of gray hair and that her skin was quite smooth, with only a few spots.

My father left the bird alone, and Lilly looked him over, the way mothers scrutinize their sons when they come back from some faraway place or, in his case, from prison. And then she asked him whether he had gotten enough food.

"You got skinny, Jimmy," she said, and he said he had gained weight, pointing to his stomach. Then he pointed to me and said, "This is my kid, Brad." She looked at me and nodded and said that the last time she had seen me was when I was a baby.

That was right. At the time, we had still been living in Memphis, and she wasn't living in the retirement home yet, but I couldn't remember her.

Fortunately, we didn't stay long. We probably would have stayed longer if there had been something to talk. But what could my father have told her, anyway? Though I was only a kid, I knew he was living a life he didn`t want to talk about. Womanizing. Jail time. Motels. Truck stops. Highways leading to nowhere, certainly not back to Winstel. Those weren't things one wants to share with one's mother.

Lilly only said that, in a way, she was glad not having to live with her son Lewis and his wife Lizette anymore. She kept assuring my father that she was happy there. That the nursing staff was thoughtful. That she was getting first-class medical care, in case, she should fall ill one day. That the garden was lush and colorful and that considering she'd only been there for half a year, she had already adjusted to the place pretty well.

I don't know why I already felt that she didn't belong there. I would have loved to have taken her by the hand and led her outside, into the sunshine.

She was sixty-four at the time, but for me, that didn't mean anything. I couldn't think back sixty-four years. Today, I find that much easier. World War I was drawing to an end when Lilly was born — 1918. People were celebrating. Peace was supposed to last forever.

On the way out, I saw the man in the wheelchair steel coffee from the farter. The old woman had fallen asleep too, and the other one stole a piece of cake from her as she snored. At that moment I understood that it was all just a game and nothing else.

I never forgot Lilly and the four old people, but I was glad that dad never picked me up again to visit her. Once in a while, I thought about her, before falling asleep, or when I saw old people somewhere in Winstel. But each time my thoughts turned to her, I tried to quickly forget her again because it was a strangely desolate feeling to think of her and the retirement home and old people in general.

Sometimes, when I thought of Lilly, I was sure that I could never do anything like this to my mother. I mean, stick her in a home and let her rot slowly, as my father did. I cannot say that I have exceptionally loving sentiments toward my mother, but I would never abandon her. As far as my father was concerned, I didn't have a clear picture of him at the time. He seemed to be never there when I needed him. He was always off knocking around with somebody. Mom called him a skirt-chaser, and sometimes she called him worse, really ugly stuff, but I often wished that he would come back and take me away from Winstel, to some other place where he was living in an RV, anywhere. And I wished he would have told me stories of his life, of the Vietnam War, of his women, of the junk cars that he put back together single-handedly until they stood there like new. I wanted to look like him, comb my hair exactly like him, parted to the left, with a pomade puff like Elvis had when mom wasn't yet my mother. And I was overjoyed when he brought me his worn-out shoes and said I could wear them one day when I was less likely to pee on them.

CHAPTER 4
ALESHA, BABY

I had just turned fifteen when I met Alesha. A whole bunch of long and boring years had gone by since my first visit with Lilly. It was around the time Mrs. Ledbetter, while crying, told me about the twins, and Mr. Ledbetter decided that he needed to protect his daughter Hanna from me and my naughty desire to sleep with her someday.

Mom had arranged a party for Lilly's sixty-ninth birthday, but she got the year wrong. It should have been her seventieth, but my mom figured it wasn't a big deal.

The party took place at our house in Winstel, and mom had invited everybody, including my father. He was living somewhere in California at the time, with a girlfriend, whom he didn't bring along because he didn't want to show her to us. He even had money for a change, probably from his girlfriend. He brought us presents. A collection of matchbox cars for Mitch, and a CD player for me. I was wearing father's shoes and was mighty proud.

"Where'd you get those stupid shoes you're wearing?" he asked, surprised.

"They're used to be yours," I said, feeling glum.

We celebrated with Lilly that day. That was the last time we were all together. The last time father danced with Lilly and Uncle Lewis kissed my mom on her cheek. Everything was all right that day I'll never forget as long as I live because suddenly Alesha was there and

37

I had never seen a more beautiful girl. Well, I didn't exactly know whether she was still a girl or already a woman. But I saw how dad almost freaked out when she came along with her long legs in a red mini skirt and a thin blouse, through which her bra was visible. Her hair danced around her face as if it had a life of its own. She laughed and danced with Lilly. And then she danced with my mom and my brother. I almost fainted when she came toward me and took me by the arm. She taught me how to dance. No kidding. She showed me every step, and I stared at her long, naked legs down to her small feet, which stuck in pointed shoes with high, pencil-thin heels. And sometimes, when we got close, she touched my head with her breasts, just like that, kissed me and laughed, and I got so dizzy I had to hold onto her.

Hanna was also there. And so were the Ledbetter's, because my mom had high respect for Mr. Ledbetter, as well as a small loan with the bank, which she was only able to pay off sporadically.

I felt Mr. Ledbetter watching me curiously, and I could see that he had the most cunning thoughts while watching me dance with Alesha. Presumably, he recognized in me nothing else but a lust-driven teenager. Well, he got that right. While watching how enchanted I was by Alesha, he probably intended to use this to erect barriers between me and his daughter, Hanna, but on the other hand, he got mad because I wasn't paying enough attention to her.

Alesha was from Dickens, the county seat, and my mother knew her from work. She was a nurse, and one would notice that immediately because she got on especially well with Lilly and the other older people, but she didn't seem to take heed of my father. He didn't take that well for long, so he got drunk. And when he was utterly wasted — I mean wasted as one can be still standing — he stumbled to her and just grabbed her by the wrist.

"Now we're going to dance, baby," I heard him say, and she told him to let go of her wrist. He laughed and put an arm around her waist. I saw how she was leaning her upper body backward when he wanted to kiss her. And then she belted him one, quick as lightning, and so deftly that he had no chance to duck. He staggered and fell over. Lewis helped him to his feet, and Lilly demanded that he apologize to Alesha.

And he did. With a bow.

"I didn't mean it like that," he said and laughed. And the matter would have been forgotten. However, it was not forgotten, because my father could not forget Alesha. Even though he made a serious effort to leave her alone during the party, something wasn't right anymore. After dinner, I disappeared into my room and pulled out the shoebox I kept there with old photos, including a few pictures of Lilly from way back.

I was looking at the photos when Hanna stepped into my room. Without knocking. I quickly put the pictures away.

"What are you doing up here?" she asked.

"Nothing much," I said.

"Why don't you come downstairs and dance with me?"

"Because your father's eyes are glued to my back."

"Ah, now it's my father standing between us, Bradley?"

I was silent. Hanna threw herself on the bed.

"I want to make you happy, Bradley," she said in a strangely sticky voice. "Come on and kiss me."

I bent over her, and we kissed, and she wrapped her arms around me and almost choked me.

That was the first time she had come on to me in such a wild way, and I started to undo her blouse. She didn't stop me until I wanted to push up her bra. As always, when I was almost exploding inside, she pushed my hand away from her and sat up.

"Not now, Bradley," she said. But, as if by chance, she put her hand on my trousers. I was laying still, my penis hard as a rock. And she squeezed it, which she had never done before. Then she laughed and jumped off the bed.

I kept lying on the bed while she adjusted her bra and buttoned her blouse. Then she went downstairs, and I was lying on the bed thinking of Alesha. It was like a dream. Unreal. She just couldn't be the way I imagined her. So keen on me and so seductive. After all, she was a few years older than me and probably not interested in getting involved with a fourteen-year-old boy. But I couldn't stop letting myself be seduced by her. In the end, I went to the bathroom and jerked off, the image of her in my mind. I didn't have to try hard to imagine that she was with me.

Later, I pulled the shoebox out from under my bed again and took out the photos.

One showed a small house standing somewhere on the

edge of a cornfield, with a man I didn't know. But the name written on the back was one I had heard several times at our house: JB.

CHAPTER 5
BASTARDS ARE BLACK

JB's story began long before I was in this world.

I heard about him for the first time when I was about six. I remember that it was when my mom got into a bad fight with my dad before my brother was born. I was in bed, trying to sleep.

I'll never forget that fight. The court documents said it was the first time my father hit my mother. I found the papers by accident in an envelope my mom kept hidden in the living room cupboard.

Father came home late, but not as late as he often did. And he wasn't drunk, either. But my mom smelled something on him that drove her nuts. She called my dad a bastard. I heard it clearly, even though I had buried my head under the blanket. I always got into a sort of panic whenever they were fighting.

"I hate you, you bastard! You are just like your father, JB!"

My ears heard that as clearly as if mom was screaming at me, but I didn't understand.

Then my father struck out, and my mom yelled, and my father yelled, and all of a sudden there was a deadly silence in the house, and I thought they'd killed each other. I sneaked out of the room, fearing the worst. But my mom wasn't dead. She only had a black eye and was sitting in front of the TV, watching some Elvis movie, with one eye covered by an ice pack.

"Hey," I said, and she jumped. Then she waved me

over to her, and when I sat down next to her, she put her arm around me and started crying.

I asked her who JB was, but she just cried that much harder and put her other arm around me and held me tight. She said she had said something to dad that she shouldn't have, and that she was ashamed. She told me not to worry about dad because she'd make up for it when he came home.

But my father didn't come home. Mom was so angry that she sued him for assault. And a few weeks later, when he did come home, there was a hearing at the family court. From then on, our family wasn't a real family anymore, and nothing seemed ever to be right after that night.

My parents fought more often than before, but my father never touched my mother again. When they were fighting, I often heard the name JB mentioned. Which isn't a proper name really, just two letters, which I didn't know at the time were the initials of John Bradley. I didn't know who he was, but from then on, my mind was preoccupied with JB. Later, when father wasn't living with us anymore, and mom was pregnant with Mitch, I asked her again who JB was. She looked at me as if I had just contracted a virus. Then she said, "You'd better never ask me about him again, son," and I never did ask her again because I didn't want to get sick.

My mom took a job as a waitress at the Triple T Truck Stop in Dickens. And Hanna Ledbetter, whom I had already fallen in love with in first grade, had a whole bunch of zits on her face and wore a bra stuffed with foam rubber padding. She also played offensive midfield for the Sidewinders, a girls' soccer team.

My last name was still Fletcher. Sometime later, after Mitch was born, my mom brought a man home. His name was McDelcott. She told me, "This is Mr. McDelcott; he's your new father."

To which I gruffly replied: "I don't need one because I've already got one."

McDelcott didn't seem to mind. He had little Mitch who was still too little to know who his father was.

I don't know exactly when mother reminded me that Mitch and I also had a grandmother, who was quite old and possibly had a small fortune, which she couldn't take to her grave because shrouds don't have pockets. That is how she explained it to Mitch and me. Much to McDelcott's disapproval. He didn't dare contradict my mom or chime in with his advice, though. He only sat there with a displeased expression.

"Brad, didn't you always want to know who JB was? Why don't you go to her and just ask her? I'm sure Lilly is dying to tell you about JB."

At first, I thought I hadn't heard right. I figured Lilly would be that old she wouldn't even remember we existed, and I was almost certain she wouldn't want to know anything about us.

My father used to be her favorite son, until he brought us to Texas and her to Memphis, more or less leaving her in the care of my Uncle Lewis, her youngest son. Lewis sent her to the retirement home later, because his wife, Lizette, didn't want to have the old lady in her house anymore. It was a typical family story, as I saw it.

I told my mom that I didn't remember Lilly, which, of course, was a lie. She laughed and said I got along so well with people and didn't need to fear her.

"Bradley, I know Lilly thinks very highly of you."

I had no idea what she meant. Who was I, anyway? A nerd who neither played baseball or football in high school, but who watched the girls play soccer because Hanna was one of them, and who read tons of books written by weird authors like Cormac McCarthy or Tom Spanbauer. My father also believed I was an awkward intellectual who sat down on the toilet to pee in order not to pee on the toilet seat, as he did. That was simply beyond him. For him, it was almost like a betrayal of manhood, whatever that was supposed to mean. He stood there, watching me pee; and to see me like that, sitting on the toilet seat, caused him real agony, so he ordered me to pee standing up from then on. And when I tried, I peed on my shoes. Fortunately, they were not yet his shoes.

"You'll get it right someday, kid" he comforted me.

I was wearing his shoes when I visited Lilly alone for the first time.

That was after the birthday party. Father had disappeared again without a trace. Alesha wasn't living in Dickens anymore, either. A rumor was making the rounds that she had moved to Memphis with a new lover, a veterinarian from Tennessee. She had moved to Memphis, of all places, but this honestly didn't have anything to do with the decision I made to visit Lilly. At the time, Hanna and I had fallen out because I had told her that I didn't feel like going to college in Texas after high school in three years and that I'd much rather go to Chicago.

I just decided to go to Memphis. By myself.

My mom praised me for my courage and bought me a duffle bag at the junk store in Dickens.

"The old lady will probably leave you her fortune one day," my mom said when she saw me off.

"I don't need a fortune," I replied, unaware at that point what sort of gift I'd receive from Lilly.

CHAPTER 6
ENCOUNTER IN BATON ROUGE

I was fifteen, and there I was, traveling on my own to Memphis. It was during that visit that Lilly told me about JB for the first time.

It was a beautiful autumn day, no clouds in the sky, and the afternoon was so warm that I wore shorts and a short-sleeved shirt. Lilly wore a light blue dress, with a pattern of dark blue flowers, white socks, and new shoes. Her hair was silver and shone like an angel's halo. I had come straight from my Uncle Lewis's house, but she didn't ask me about him or his family. She just looked up at me and said: "Bradley, I'm going to tell you a story that I haven't told anybody yet."

To be honest, I had been expecting it. All that time spent traveling there; I had only been thinking how I would ask Lilly about JB. Then she said that in her entire life there had been only one man she truly loved.

"JB," I said.

She smiled.

"Come, Bradley, let's go down and sit in the sun."

Down in the garden, we sat on a bench, and in the warmth and the sunlight, Lilly blossomed like a flower after a long, harsh winter.

"Even though you don't look like JB, you remind me of him," she said. "It's the eyes, the life in them. So much life. So much desire and joy. I thought that nothing could hold him back, but I didn't know how easy it would be to destroy everything."

Of course, I had no idea what she was talking about, and she realized that and leaned back, so her face was in the sun. She smiled and closed her eyes, and she sat next to me like that for several minutes, hands in her lap and a soft smile on her face. I thought she had fallen asleep, and I touched her hand. Without opening her eyes, she said, "Yes, one day, I will see him again, and it will be the most beautiful day of my life."

"Where is he?" I asked as if we would only have to drive somewhere to visit him.

"I believe he is not with us anymore," she said.

"You mean he's dead?" I asked.

"That may well be. He was quite a bit older than me, seven or eight years indeed. In any case, he already had a few gray hairs here and there, when I first met him. That was down in Baton Rouge. I was supposed to go to college there, and my father and mother went with me to take a look at the college. I was seventeen at the time, and he was twenty-five or twenty-six. I saw him at a restaurant, and the second I saw him my heart wanted to burst. I couldn't do anything but look at him again and again. We had a meal at this restaurant, my parents and I.

I can still remember my father's face. He never took his eyes off me and, of course, immediately noticed what was going on. He didn't say anything, though. He was only watching me and, once in a while, he would look over to the smaller room, I guess you would call it a bar or a tavern. I remember it had sawdust on the floor. This room was separated from our dining room because only whites were allowed in our area, and only blacks in the other. JB was one of the few blacks; he was sitting at one of the tables with another black man and his wife, and he looked across just once when I was watching, and my father noticed that our eyes met, and he also knew what it meant. He offered to change seats with my mother so that I would be able to sit with my back to the other room, but I told him that I was happy where I was sitting.

"I probably would never have seen JB again if my father hadn't been so stupid as to ask the waiter about the young black man sitting there in that other room, talking and laughing with his friends, and who now and again looked through the opening of a sliding door and made my heart race.

"'That is JB Swift,' said the waiter.

"'And who is JB Swift?' my father asked.

"The waiter thought for a minute and then said that, in spite of his young age, JB Swift was a bit of a legend already, especially here in Louisiana, but also in Mississippi, Arkansas, and Tennessee, and even in East Texas.

"'Why a legend?' asked my father.

"'JB Swift is a man of the blues,' explained the waiter.

"My father knew what the 'blues' was, even though no one was allowed to listen to blues on the radio in our house, because the blues was 'nigger music,' as people called it in the old days before the war, and nigger music was something for blacks and white trash, as we called those lower-class people who didn't fit in with our society, even though their skin was white.

"As the waiter left, I feared he would close the sliding door behind him, but he left it open. I saw him walk to the table in the other room, bending over and whispering something to JB Swift, who immediately looked in our direction and smiled. While I lowered my head, I noticed my father's grim face and I heard him growl, 'Bold little black fucker.' I was shocked. Never before I heard my father saying anything like that arrogant and derogatory, I thought he must have lost his mind. After a while, I raised my head, but I made sure not to look straight at the young man again.

"And JB Swift? Well, he left the bar before we had finished our meal. But he didn't go through the door designated for blacks. He came through our dining room, forbidden to him and his like. And he was heading straight to our table, and I saw how sweat broke out on my father's forehead. My mother, who was unable to see JB because she was sitting with her back toward the other dining room, gave me a nervous look. I barely dared look at him, but I saw him come toward our table and, Bradley, you won't believe this, but my heart stopped beating when he stood at our table. He was wearing a brown suit with subtle pinstripes and a hat and white-brown shoes that were the height of fashion in those days, and a dark red rose in his lapel.

He took off his hat and held it with one hand behind his back.

"'Sir,' he said to my father, 'Sir, allow me to pay my respects by giving your beautiful daughter this rose.'

"I thought my heart would stop beating, as he took the rose from his jacket and handed it to me with a radiant smile.

"And I took it. I don't know what made me take it from his hand and what prevented my father from calling the police. And I don't know why Mother didn't faint. I only know that I looked him in the eyes, and they were just like yours, Bradley. The same eyes, I tell you, and my hand trembled when I took the rose from his hand. I noticed his hand, this fine, almost delicate hand, with veins prominent on the back and long, beautiful fingers. He was wearing a golden wristwatch, and he smelled of perfume that I later learned came from Paris. As I was holding the rose in my hand, he stood up straight and apologized for having interrupted our meal, and he said, 'I hope we'll see each other again. My name is JB Swift.'

"I wanted to tell him my name, but I couldn't get a sound to pass my lips, and so off he went with a smile. He left the restaurant without looking back even once, but I knew I would see him again."

Lilly broke off. We were sitting next to each other on the bench, in the sun. After a while, she opened her eyes and took my hand into both of hers and looked at me.

"You want to know whether I ever saw him again. Right, Bradley?"

"You did see him again," I said, thinking of that night when my father hit my mom for the first and last time.

"I did see him again," said Lilly. "One year later. I hadn't forgotten him, but I hadn't been thinking of him every day. I went to college in Memphis, not in Baton

Rouge. I saved the petals of his rose, pressed between the pages of my favorite books."

I waited for her to continue her story, but she didn't. Instead, she said she would tell me about them meeting again on my next visit. She would also tell me how she first saw JB on stage with his guitar.

I told her I would come back the next day.

She smiled.

"Then I'll tell you about an exceptional day in my life, Bradley."

CHAPTER 7
LADY IN BLUE

It was a day from the past, long before I was born. For Lilly, though, it didn't seem so long ago. Lilly hadn't forgotten a single detail. She remembered things that could only have been committed to memory this clearly by somebody who, at the time, was fully aware of the day's significance.

It was a Wednesday, she had said. On the radio, there were reports about some attempts of the American people to provide necessary supplies for the people suffering in the dust bowl of the Midwest. Their suffering was boundless. Within one year, over three million people had had to leave their hometowns for the promised land of California. A wagon train of despair moved along the dusty roads toward the west. Men, women, and children — the young and the old. All Americans were called upon to participate in the humanitarian cause. They were asked to donate all they could spare: money, food, clothing, household goods, and bedding. At the time, Lilly was a freshman at Memphis College. Her father decided that Baton Rouge would not be the right environment for his daughter. Lilly was majoring in history, English, and sociology. She wanted to become a teacher. She saw her life's calling was in teaching where poor people lived; in the backcountry of Tennessee, in the remote valleys of the Appalachians and the Cumberland Mountains, or in the villages in the forests along the Natchez Trace, where schools and teachers were few and far between.

Lilly also worked while she was studying. From her father, she merely got a small contribution toward her tuition. She had to pay for food and board.

Every evening, she stacked goods in a department store warehouse on Poplar Avenue. To save money on commuting expenses, she walked. She usually got home around midnight after hours of hard work for a quarter an hour, which was the minimum wage.

On the morning of that Wednesday, she sat with her friend Mary Jane in the library, in front of a stack of books about Shakespeare. They were reading excerpts and taking notes they needed for their seminar. It was quiet in the library. There were male and female students working everywhere at the tables. Lilly remembered a boy named Phil Pollack, who had fallen asleep over his books. And she remembered Tommy Clifford who, while passing by her, whispered in her ear that he was in love with her beautiful eyes.

And then Sue came to the table and asked Mary Jane whether she would go with her to the Royal Blue Club that evening.

"I heard what they were talking about, even though I was engrossed in my reading material," said Lilly, smiling as she leaned back on the bench in the sun. It was afternoon. The sky had a thin cloud cover that day, but the sun was shining warmly, and there was no wind. Lilly looked into the distance, but her eyes were not seeing the view. She was fifty years away from me, inside memories that would never fade as long as she lived.

"Royal Blue was a name we were all familiar with in

those days. A club for blacks. Bluesmen performed there. The club, and what happened there, was often the topic of conversation. Sometimes, it even made the headlines in the papers. Even before the war, the Royal Blue was famous. The most celebrated blues musicians performed there. The place had a good reputation at one time. But now, just before the war, that was different. The police raided it almost every month. In the backrooms, gamblers and prostitutes got arrested. Money got seized and weapons found. The nastiest of rumors made the rounds. Whites no longer went there unless they belonged to that band of outsiders who consorted with blacks by night. We didn't call them blacks back then, though. We called them Negros. And some even called them niggers. A nigger was thought to be an inferior creature, not far removed from monkeys, as my father once claimed. Their music was equally disreputable. Nigger music. Hardly any radio station played it. I still remember well how my father would immediately turn off the radio when a piece got played that had even the slightest resemblance to the blues, or when a singer sang a song in a Negro-like way. We listened to the blues only secretly, in our room in the dorm, on the weekend, and when I was at Mary Jane's and her parents were gone. Mary Jane even had a few records by black musicians in a secret hiding place in her room. We would secretly dance to them because they had a unique rhythm. White music didn't have that rhythm. White music was safe. Cozy. Without life. When we danced to black music, we felt naughty. We felt our young hearts beat madly inside of us. It was not only because to us the black music was forbidden, which made it even more appealing, of course. At home, we were well-behaved girls who never did anything wrong. As soon as we were alone, our parents would not have recognized us. Nonetheless, I would never have dreamed of going to the Royal Blue. I wouldn't even have dared go anywhere near it because I understood I would ruin my reputation as a good girl if somebody saw me there.

"'Who is playing this evening, then?' I heard Mary Jane ask, and in a way, I still wasn't paying attention, as I was busy with Hamlet.

"'JB,' Sue said and tore me out of the middle of Hamlet so suddenly that I bit through the pencil I had in my mouth.

"Sue and Mary Jane stared at me as if I'd been invisible a second ago, and they were just seeing me after the loud snap of my pencil.

"'Where did you come from?' whispered Sue. 'Sorry if I disturbed you studying.'

"And Mary Jane laughed. 'You haven't bitten through that pencil, have you, Lilly?'

"'No, my teeth did it all by themselves,' I said barely moving my lips and looking all around me. Luckily, nobody was nearby who could have blabbed to one of the professors or my father.

"'Did I hear right that you want to go to the Royal Blue tonight, Sue?'

"'This was not for your ears, Lilly,' said Sue. 'You'll probably have to work.'

"'I did hear it, though,' I said stubbornly. 'And I also heard the name you mentioned. JB Swift. I have never told anybody, not even you, Mary Jane, but I know JB.'

"They stared at me, and their eyes almost popped out of their heads. Mary Jane even gasped like a fish out of water.

"'Don't talk lies, Lilly! How would you, of all people, know a bluesman?'

"I told them the story of how I had met JB, and at first, they didn't want to believe me; they even tried to joke about it and ridicule my story, but I didn't bother me, not until Sue challenged me not to go to work that night. 'Call them and tell them you're sick. Stomach thing, or whatever. You ate something that didn't agree with you. That could easily happen with the muck they feed us here in the cafeteria.'

"'If what you tell us is true, then we'll see whether he'll recognize you,' said Mary Jane, who was a bit annoyed because I had never told her about my secret.

"All afternoon I thought about whether I should go to the Royal Blue or work. It was clear what my sense of duty demanded. I was confused and was getting so nervous that my face broke out in red blotches, around the nose, and on my forehead. It looked terrible, and I didn't want to be seen like that. Apart from that, I didn't know what I should wear. I had no idea what it was like there. All I knew was that it was a disreputable tavern where there was a lot of drinking and smoking, and a person's life could be in danger among all those black performers and pimps. I simply couldn't decide. I watched Mary Jane and Sue getting ready, with lots of makeup and curlers in their hair. The whole time they urged me to make a decision. They took hours in the bathroom and front of the mirror. And finally, they were ready, and I was still sitting on the bed, crying because I was utterly beside myself. I hadn't even called the warehouse where I worked.

"Mary Jane and Sue went alone. Only when they were gone, I got up and took a quick bath without getting my hair wet. Then, I put on a dress I had sewn myself; I liked the way it looked on me particularly well. And I put on lipstick and brushed my hair before I carefully combed it and fixed it in a knot at the back of my neck. Still, without real courage, I looked at myself in the mirror. My eyes looked a bit as if I had been crying. Apart from that, nobody would be able to tell that I was jumbled up inside and that I was afraid of going to the Royal Blue.

"It was already dark, and I took the bus into the city and got off two stops early. And then, with my heart pounding, I slipped through the dark back streets to Beale Street and the Royal Blue. Some people were standing by the door, in the blue neon light, all blacks. One woman wore a fiery red hat and fiery red shoes with unbelievably high heels. There were men, wearing dark suits with white shirts and ties. They smoked cigarettes and cigars while talking to each other, pushing each other around. And the woman was hanging onto a large man, and he put an arm around her and held her tight. She laughed, and he let her take a drag from his cigarette. I noticed the music coming from the club, the sound of a piano, the bright voice of a female singer, drums, and a bass, and my heart started to beat even faster. Everything I saw and heard confirmed the rumors people spread in the city about the Royal Blue Club. This place was not for me, and I was aware of that; it was nothing but a sinful temptation. Nonetheless, I remained there in the darkness of a side street, watching the people by the entrance, mesmerized, waiting and hoping they would finally go inside. But they didn't go inside, and I didn't know what to do, when, all of a sudden, someone spoke to me.

"'If you want, I'll take you inside with me, little girl,' said a man. I was startled, as I hadn't felt or seen anyone nearby. Now, someone was standing there, thin as a rake and short, with a checked jacket and a red bow tie under his pointy chin. His hair glistened from the pomade he used to plaster it down on his head. 'They call me Crazy Legs because I can dance like nobody else,' he said. 'When I look at you lopsidedly, don't make anything of it. My left eyelid doesn't work properly.'

"I can't tell you, Bradley, why I trusted this little man, but I did. I went with him; even though I knew what I was doing wasn't right. He paid for me at the door, told the cashier I was his girlfriend and that I was twenty-one. The cashier closed one eye and said it was all right, and another man, broad-shouldered and with a banged up face opened a heavy door for us.

"'Crazy Legs, tell the little girl what to do if the cops show up,' the man at the door murmured to my companion. And then, we stood in a thick cloud of smoke, brightly lit by a spotlight that illuminated a small stage. The people I could see were no more than silhouettes moving in the fog, blending into each other, separating again, constantly changing form, as if they were figures in a mysterious shadow play.

"Dazed as I was, my heart pounding, Crazy Legs led me around and introduced me to more people than I could keep track of. I have long since forgotten who they were. Then I danced with him, and he moved smoothly around me, contorting his flexible body in all sorts of directions. Then, he laughed and took me by the arm and kissed me when I didn't expect it. I wanted to stop dancing, but he wouldn't let me go, and other people surrounded us, laughing women in swirling dresses, and men in fancy suits. Suddenly, I caught a quick glance of Sue dancing with a young black man, in a close embrace. Then I saw Mary Jane sitting at a table raising her glass, her face illuminated by the light from a lamp, and I noticed that her lipstick was smudged.

"And then I saw JB. He stood at the bar with other men and women. As I saw him, from behind, it was as if he sensed my glance. He turned around abruptly and spotted me among the others. My heart stopped, and I was happy to have Crazy Legs to hold onto. Otherwise, I would probably have fainted and fallen. I tried not to look in his direction while I was dancing. I tried to avoid his gaze, but I didn't manage to. I felt drawn to him as if by magic, and when I turned, and we would lose sight of each other for a second, I would immediately look for him again. I found him in the clouds of blue smoke and the pink light of the lamps. I found him among the other shadows, his gaze hanging on me as if he feared he would lose me.

"The music abruptly came to an end. Crazy Legs wanted to lead me back to the table where we had been sitting, but he noticed something wasn't right. He saw JB standing at the bar, and he murmured something I couldn't make out. The people around us gradually left the dance floor. In the end, we were standing there alone, Crazy Legs and me. He wanted to take me by the arm, but then JB put out his cigarette in the ashtray, left the bar and came over to us just as he had approached our table in Baton Rouge. He seemed to see only me.

"I heard Mary Jane call my name. She had noticed me when most of the people had turned their attention on JB and me, and maybe also to Crazy Legs. And there he was, standing in front of me, tall and slender in his stylish suit, with a rose in the lapel. This time, he wasn't wearing a hat, and his hair was all shiny and carefully parted on the left. He stopped in front of me. I held my breath. I could only stand there, looking into his eyes, and I knew there was no way out.

"Bradley, one day, if you are lucky, you will experience such a moment, and you will think it could last an eternity because everything around you drops away.

"I stood there, and he took me by the arm and said something to Crazy Legs. He told him to leave me alone or something like that. I heard Crazy Legs say that he was the one who brought me here and that I was his girlfriend, but JB didn't respond. He led me to his friends at the bar and introduced me to them.

"'This is Lilly,' he said. 'We met a year ago in Baton Rouge, and we haven't seen each other since. Lilly doesn't know yet that I've been waiting, for a whole year, for this day, when I could see her again. Today is the day of my life.'

"They all laughed, and he laughed with them, and they shook my hand, and the woman said that I shouldn't take what JB said too seriously, but JB turned to me and took me by the shoulders. He looked deep into my eyes and said, 'Every word I said is the truth, Lilly.'

"He led me to the dance floor. We danced, and he told me about his life, joked about his friends and himself, and once, he asked me why I had come to the club. I admitted that I had come because I had heard his name and that I wanted to hear him sing and play the guitar.

"'You hadn't forgotten me either, Lilly?' he asked. I had to laugh. How could I have forgotten him? His name was in the newspapers. Shortly after we met in Baton Rouge, he produced his first record in New York. He had played in the old Lafayette Theater there. And he had been in Chicago, and in San Francisco. Although he was still a young man and only at the beginning of his career, they already called him a legend, and that amused him.

"'One would think I was already dead,' he said while we danced. At the time, neither of us knew how close to the truth this was or what would happen in the days that followed.

"We were happy to have found each other again.

That evening, we were probably the happiest people in the Royal Blue, perhaps even the most fortunate in the world. We believed that nothing could destroy our happiness. Nothing could separate us again.

"After we danced, JB went up to the podium and picked up his guitar. It became eerily quiet in the Royal Blue. Most of the people looked up at him, but some looked at me. I felt their eyes, and I bowed my head to avoid them. I would have preferred to leave, but I couldn't because I wanted to hear him play. I raised my head and saw Mary Jane and Sue. Mary Jane gestured to me furtively, and then JB stepped out of the spotlight to the edge of the podium. He bowed slightly, looking for me in the half darkness, found me among his friends standing at the bar and said, 'My friends, I have found my happiness again in the Royal Blue.'

That's all he said, but everyone knew what he meant. They clapped their hands and called out their good luck wishes as if it were his birthday.

"'This song,' he said, 'that I'm singing for the first time in public today, I dedicate to Lilly. It's called Lady in Blue. I wrote the song after I met Lilly, and I saved it for today.'

"It was so quiet in the Royal Blue that one could have heard a pin drop. He sat on a stool and began to play. Just like that. As if he always knew that one day he would sing this song to me. And there I stood, down in the half dark, and felt the tears welling in my eyes and my heart threatened to burst with joy."

CHAPTER 8
THE LEGEND

I was supposed to return to Winstel the next day, but I called my mother and told her I would stay another day or two in Memphis. I didn't say anything about the story Lilly was telling me. It probably wouldn't have interested her anyway. She only asked if Lilly had revealed anything to me about her financial situation, and when I told her she hadn't, she sounded disappointed.

I also told Uncle Lewis that I would like to stay a few more days, and he said it was okay, but I sensed that his hospitality, in a way, had already come to an end. They told me of their weekend plans, of going to see some old friends who lived somewhere in Louisiana. I told them I would be returning to Winstel the next day.

But I didn't. I packed my things very early the next day and had Uncle Lewis drive me to the Greyhound Station, but when he was gone, I left the station and called up the retirement home.

The receptionist told me that Lilly was in the garden, but that she already had asked about me several times. I dropped off my duffel bag at the luggage deposit, got a ticket with a number on it, and walked to Beale Street.

Even back then, Beale Street's glory days were long gone. Only a few of the old restaurants, clubs, dance halls and bars remained. In the meantime, the city got some of the houses renovated in their old looks, mainly for the tourists. No doubt, things were happening here at night, but now it was daylight. The few old buildings looked as if they were falling apart, the walls were full of cracks, and most of the doors and windows were boarded up. Except for a few tourists, there was hardly anyone around. Where the marketplace had been, there now stood a memorial statue of the great W.C. Handy with his trumpet. A man with a broom was sweeping the sidewalk and shoveling the trash into a small handcart. The man was black. I asked him about the Royal Blue. He stood up straight, sized me up for a few seconds, and then looked down the street.

"Well, what do you want there, son?" he asked without looking at me.

"Have you ever heard about JB Swift?" I responded.

"JB Swift?" He took a deep breath as if it were more of an effort for him to rummage around in his memory than to sweep the street. He seemed to see something hidden from my eyes. Then, he returned his gaze to me and nodded.

"Yeah, I remember JB," he said. "They called him 'The Legend.' As if he were one of the old ones."

"Did you know him?"

"Everybody knew him." He laid his broom diagonally across the handcart and pointed to the corner of the street. "It happened over there," he said. "I was a little boy in those days, five or six, and I delivered newspapers to earn a few pennies. That was the time of the great drought. Every day, the papers wrote about it. About all those people who went west, leaving behind Farmland that looked like a sandy desert. That's when it happened, what they later called a murder, although it wasn't one.

I saw it with my own eyes, son. Later, the cops asked me about what I'd seen. I told them, even though they must have seen it themselves because some of them were standing there on the street when JB and the girl came out. I told them I'd seen how they were waiting for them, five or six of them. One of them was one of the niggers we called 'rats' because they were always slinking around the darkest corners at night. They all stood over there, between the two doors. The one door led to the pool hall where they played billiards. The other door was the entrance to Frank's Café. They were waiting for him there. He was sitting with his girl in Frank's Café, but I didn't know that. I saw the men standing over there, and they acted as if everything was hunky-dory, but I didn't like what I saw. I saw how one of them was holding a baseball bat hidden behind his back, and I thought, 'Hey, what's going on here. What does someone like him want to do with a baseball bat here in the middle of the city?' And while I thought that, they came out of Frank's, JB, and the girl. One of the men stepped into his path and asked him for a light. As JB let go of the girl and reached into his jacket pocket for his lighter, they began to shove him around. He raised both his hands and said that he wanted to go on his way with his girl in peace, but they didn't let him walk on. And then JB lost control. He hit one of them right in the face with his fist, and the others drew back. For a few seconds, they all were paralyzed, and JB probably thought he could walk away, but then the baseball bat hit him in the spine, and he went to his knees. I can still see it clearly, how he went down on his knees with a look of disbelief. I heard his girl scream, and two of the men grabbed her and pulled her into the street. JB was kneeling on the ground, and the one with the baseball bat screamed at him and then swung at JB again. JB tried to block the blow with his arm. The baseball bat struck his arm, and I learned later that the blow broke it, very close to the wrist. I didn't hear what the one with the baseball bat said to JB afterward, but JB just stared at him. As the man with the bat turned around, ready to walk away, JB suddenly had a revolver in his hand. I had no idea where from he got the gun. It was just all of a sudden in his hand, and then a shot rang out. I saw a flame coming out of the muzzle, like fire, and the man with the baseball bat got knocked forward. He staggered several steps into the street before his legs gave way under him. I think he tried to grab hold of something, but there was nothing to hold on to, so he simply went down in the middle of the street, not thirty paces from here. He fell lengthwise onto his face, and they later said he was already dead when he hit the asphalt. However, I saw clearly, as he was lying on the ground, how he raised his head and moved one arm as if he wanted to try to get up one more time."

The street sweeper had spoken in one go for such a long time that he was winded. Now, deep in thought, he shook his head and breathed deeply.

"No," he said. "It didn't work; he couldn't get up anymore."

I stared at the spot where it had happened. Any trace had disappeared a long time ago. Loose trash blew in by the wind and strewn all over the potholed street. Paper cups. Strips of paper. Glass shards glittered everywhere. Cigarette butts. An old shoe in the gutter where the man hadn't cleaned up yet. A piece of wood from a crate.

I stared across at the old buildings. One of the doors hung on its hinges. The other entrance was boarded up.

"Today, it's all forgotten," the man said as he reached for his broom again. "Most of these people are dead. JB Swift died in prison. And the girl…"

He left the sentence unfinished and began to sweep.

"Is there anybody else here who was alive then?"

"Nobody, I believe. But if only the houses over there could talk, boy, they'd make your head spin."

"I'll ask them," I said, laughing.

"Just be careful, son. The spirits of this street won't let go of you again in a hurry. They used to say that when white folks came here, they wanted to be black afterward. It's better for you to stay white, son, even today."

I slowly walked on, walked to the street corner and opened the door, which at one time had been the entrance to Frank's Café. Worn out linoleum covered the floor. In some places, big patches had been ripped up, and the floorboards were showing, grooved, blackboards with glue and small pieces of linoleum floor sticking to them. The window was shattered, and the tin ceiling hung down, and where the stove had once been, the wall scorched. A small door led into the room that must have been the kitchen, but nothing more served as a reminder that this once had been Frank's Café. I went outside and looked for the street sweeper, but couldn't see him anywhere. I stopped on the sidewalk. That was where they had been waiting. I memorized everything and tried to imagine how it all might have happened. I saw how the men dragged Lilly across the street, and I saw the little boy on the other side of the street, with a cap lopsidedly on his head and a bag full of newspapers. And I saw JB go to his knees, stricken by the first blow, blocking the second with his left arm, as his right hand reached into his pocket for his revolver. And I heard Lilly scream, saw how she tried to break loose, saw the shock in the newspaper boy's eyes, heard the cry of pain as a bone in JB's arm broke, and finally, I heard the shot.

I didn't know why it had happened. Why did JB carry a revolver, and why were the men waiting for him here at this place?

A patrol car with two cops slowly drove by. The driver was white, and the other was black. Both of them looked in my direction. The patrol car slowed down, then stopped. They got out. The black cop put on his cap and came up to me.

"What are you doing here, kid?" he said, looking me over through his sunglasses.

"Nothing much," I said.

He eyed me suspiciously.

"You're not from here, are you?"

"No."

"Where are you from?"

"Texas."

"Are you by yourself?"

"No, sir. My uncle lives here. And my grandmother."

"And what are you doing here?"

"Somebody told me what happened here," I said. "Do you know what happened here?"

"Here? Nothing's happened here for years." He looked around as if he suspected something had changed without him noticing it. "No, nothing's happened. They talk about renovating Beale Street. Souvenir stores and new blues bars. All new, kid. Tinsel and glitter. Only rats are still living in the old buildings over there. In those early days, things were different. This street was the birthplace of the blues. The wind carried the songs from the cotton fields of the South here, and from those songs came the blues."

I looked at him, not at all surprised that he too felt compelled to tell me more than I had asked for.

"In nineteen hundred and nine, W.C. Handy played his first blues here. In his honor, the city built a monument over there in the old marketplace."

He was not finished with his history lesson, pointed across to an open area where a few tourists were milling around as if they got lost.

"In the olden days, this was a great place to be, kid. Before the war. The great ones played here. And also the musician's nobody remembers the many forgotten ones. There was a time when people in Memphis were proud of this street and the music that originated here. The first record studios moved in. Sun Records. Elvis. Jerry Lee Lewis. And, of course, the great black blues guys like B.B. King. Soon it wasn't anymore as it used to be. So, the studios got out and moved elsewhere. The old blues musicians didn't return either. And everything here started to crumble. The rats came, and they stayed. One store after another closed down. The houses were falling apart. Nobody wanted to live here anymore, and this has been nothing but a ghost town for a long time. This street is full of memories. Sometimes, old people come here looking for traces of the past. Something that got stuck in their head, something they vaguely remember. But you seem too young to have those memories, kid."

I listened to him without daring to interrupt him. When he got done, he looked at me, trying to figure me out.

"My grandfather shot a man here who had beaten him with a baseball bat," I said.

"Your grandfather?"

"JB Swift."

The cop took a deep breath just like the street sweeper had done earlier on.

"The Legend," he said. "A master guitar player with a great passion for the blues. You want to know what happened to him."

I nodded and wanted to leave, but he followed me and held me back by the arm.

"Where are you going, kid?"

"Visit my grandmother."

"If you like, I'll take you to Sara."

"Who's that?"

"Sara Carter. She's the daughter of Professor Sam Carter, and she runs a small bookstore not far from here. She was born here, and she grew up here. She knows this street as nobody else does. I'm sure she'll gladly give you some answers."

"I'll go there tomorrow. Now, I have an appointment with my grandmother. I don't want to keep her waiting."

"Where is she?"

"In an old folks' home."

"Which one?"

"Harvest Moon."

"Okay, we'll drive you there. What's your name, anyway?"

"Bradley McDelcott." I lied, not wanting to give him my real name, Bradley Fletcher.

"I'm Officer Smart, and my partner, the white guy behind the wheel, that's Officer O'Rourke."

The driver of the patrol car was older than the black man. "What's with him?" he asked.

"We're taking him to his grandmother."

"To his grandmother?"

"He's searching for the ghosts, Tim. His grandfather was JB Swift."

"JB Swift?"

"One of us, Tim," the black man explained, laughing. "A bluesman."

"And then there was Elvis and rock 'n' roll," said the driver. "Ask Elvis if you think I'm pulling your string."

"Elvis is dead too," Officer O'Rourke said.

"Without the blues, there would not be any Elvis or rock 'n' roll, that's all I say."

CHAPTER 9
JB'S GIRL

Lilly was waiting for me in the garden. She sat slumped on the bench we had sat on the day before. When she saw me and recognized me, she quickly sat up straight and stretched her hand out to me.

"There you finally are," she said. "You know, I would have never believed I could ever again wait for someone with so much longing."

"I'm sorry. There was something I had to take care of," I said. "If you want to, we could go out and have lunch together." I had assumed that she would turn down my suggestion, but I was wrong. Her eyes lit up, and she pressed my hand and told me that she would love to. Then she called for Rhonda.

"My grandson and I are going to lunch," Lilly proudly proclaimed.

We went to the nearest McDonald's. Photos of old blues musicians covered the walls. Lilly didn't know any of them, and JB's picture wasn't among them. Later, we went down to the Mississippi, to the waterfront. And there we sat on a bench and watched the buzz, the men loading and unloading freight ships, cars driving back and forth over the Mississippi Bridge, and an old man nearby feeding the seagulls and pigeons. And without me needing to suggest it, Lilly began to talk about JB.

She talked about the happy days they'd had together, of walks along the banks of the great river, of car journeys, and of new friends she had met. Lilly gave up her job in the warehouse soon after they met again in the Royal Blue. JB demanded it. He earned enough money to give her each week the equivalent of what she would have made at the warehouse. At home, she never said she had stopped working. Instead, as often as her studies would allow, she sought out the bars and dance halls where JB was playing. Soon, she became known everywhere on Beale Street as JB's girl. That's what they called her: JB's girl. In the beginning, it bothered her, but after a while, she began to like it. Not because JB was famous and in the spotlight, but because she was proud of the happiness she found by his side. She loved him more than anything in the world. And sometimes, she said, she would wake up in the middle of the night and think of him, and she would pray for him and ask that nothing bad would happen to him. She would have been ready to die for JB if someone had asked her to do so, but she also knew that such thoughts were foolish, owing to her youth. Nobody should want to die for somebody instead of staying alive for someone.

Lilly didn't want to be without JB, and when he was on tour, she suffered. It didn't help that he called her several times a day. Only when he returned was the world right again.

I listened to her, terribly churned up inside because, since before noon that day, I knew a story that didn't fit the picture she had composed. I asked myself whether she had deliberately neglected to tell me of the shadows that she must have been aware of even back then. Someday, I thought, she will tell me of her fears and the threat she must have sensed. But instead, she told me about beautiful experiences with JB and of the world that was strange to her. I could hardly listen anymore, although I absorbed everything she said. The images she evoked became imprinted in my memory just as deeply as those that had played out in my mind on Beale Street.

The question of why JB carried a revolver was on the tip of my tongue. Who were those men in front of Frank's Café? When did her parents learn of her attraction to the black blues musician and how had her father reacted?

There were so many questions I wanted to ask, but I let her talk, let her luxuriate in her memories because I was already aware of how little time was left for her to think about the good times in her life and to conjure up once again the happiness that was so suddenly destroyed on the sidewalk outside Frank's Café.

In the afternoon, when she got tired and complained about the fading sight in her left eye, I brought her back to her room and put drops in her tired, inflamed eyes.

"The doctor thinks I should have my left eye operated on soon," she said. "I'm afraid of the operation. I never used to fear anything, but now I'm afraid of losing my eyesight. Rhonda told me it's a surgery carried out many times and that I needn't be worried, though." She paused for a few seconds and then continued, "Because I'd still have the other eye, right?" She laughed. "Among the blind, the one-eyed person is king, Bradley. One of JB's best friends, Joey Pickett, told me that. He had a glass eye."

"Did you ever hear from him again?"

"From Joey? No. Not even once. After JB went away, nobody wanted to have anything to do with me. I wouldn't have wanted it anyway. I wanted to be alone."

"Then you don't know anything about him?"

"No. I only know that he was a big star in New Orleans after the war. Crazy Legs too, by the way. I heard from him a few times. He always knew how to put himself in the limelight. I heard once that he even danced for the king and the whole royal family in London."

"Do you know where he is now?"

"No. Of course, I don't. I wanted to erase Crazy Legs from my memory, but I never quite succeeded. It's strange how we forget the people who do us good much more quickly than those who have brought us pain."

I saw her eyes close, and I stayed with her until she fell asleep. Then, I left the nursing home and started to look for Sara Carter's bookstore. As I only had a few pennies left, I walked and became somewhat lost in the city, even though I had a destination. The whole time I'd been in Memphis, I had thought of looking in the telephone directory to see if Alesha was listed there, but I couldn't remember her last name. Now, while I was walking through the streets on the way to Sara Carter's bookstore, her name came back to me; it was Prosser. Alesha Prosser.

CHAPTER 10
SEX WITH HANNA

I don't believe I'll ever forget the name again after I suddenly remembered it in Memphis. Nobody knew her in Winstel.

For me, Alesha was something like a mysterious goddess who woke me from some foggy dream I'd been stumbling through for years. And did she ever. First, she managed to drive my father crazy. And then, I began to think of nothing but sex, and when I thought of sex, it was almost all about sex with her. It was on my mind always and anywhere; at school, at home, even on the water tower, when I sat up there with Wayne. We stared at the Rimrocks, which, from a distance, looked like the long stretched out body of a woman, naked and slender, with a slight curvature at the stomach, and with breasts, which in reality were the Twin Buttes. Two bare hills where, later on, our friend Santiago Gomez would be shot down by the Border Patrol.

For a time, I wanted to forget what happened when Alesha came to Winstel for Lilly's birthday party, and above all, what happened a few weeks later. Because I didn't want to believe that, in the end, Alesha only wanted to take revenge on my dad, which I made pretty easy for her.

A few months after the birthday party, dad moved into a motel room in Dickens with Alesha. I don't know how this came about, and it surprised the hell out of me how they could get together like that after she hit him, and with him being so much older than her. At the time, I couldn't even imagine that when they were together, he must have taken her to places she'd never been. At first, the thought of it drove me crazy. My father, a fairly old man to me, with my incredible Alesha, who was more beautiful in my dreams than she was in reality. But in time, I got used to the idea that I had lost her. It didn't matter who she was with; I couldn't have her.

But Hanna was there for me. More than ever. I sensed that something would happen soon. Sex with Hanna, I thought. Not even her father could prevent this from happening because he had no idea how strong our secret desires were, nor what was going on inside me.

We often met at the pond in the Brewster Valley, and we kissed and cuddled for hours, hidden in the undergrowth. The dogwoods were so thick there that nobody could see us, not even Mitch when he came by chance to the pond to watch his tadpoles and the frogs and salamanders.

I had almost no time anymore for Wayne. Occasionally, I saw him in the distance, sitting alone on the water tower, lonelier than ever, while I was entirely preoccupied with my wild dreams.

I could no longer concentrate appropriately at school. Mr. Blanchard even called my mom and asked her if there were any problems at home. My mother said, "Tons of problems, but nothing new. Only the ones we've had since he was born." Mr. Blanchard said, "I see," although he probably didn't know what she meant.

Hanna and I, we were discovering the joy of sex.

Secretly. On a Saturday evening, after we've seen a stupid movie at the old Stardust movie theater, which was only open on weekends, we kissed in the shade of Jessie Walker's shed, behind the gas station.

Hanna wasn't wearing a bra, and she let me touch her breasts. We kissed, and we did that correctly as we've seen it in that movie, with my thick tongue in her mouth, and hers in mine and her mouth open wide that it seemed as if we wanted to swallow each other. But nothing more than that happened.

I must admit that I thought so often about what it would be like to have sex with her that I was disappointed every time it didn't happen. I believe it was always in the shadow of her father where we were trying to make love, no matter where we were hiding, and that's an uncomfortable place, of course, especially for the first time. When we would separate without it happening, I was afraid it never would until we got married, if we ever did get married.

Of course, I didn't know either what went on inside Hanna. After all, she was a girl. I simply couldn't manage to put myself into her position, but I believe that, at the time, she wasn't ready to sleep with me. Nonetheless, we groped each other expertly. When I think about it now, I believe she did it only to please me. I even sensed it back then, and I became insecure. I sensed that she was doing something she didn't want to because she was a decent girl who went to church every Sunday with her parents.

No wonder I thought more about Alesha than about Hanna when I was alone. Looking back, I guess I didn't know about how sex with Hanna would be if it came down to it. Instead, I thought only about whether sex with Hanna would be as good as the sex I had with Alesha in my imagination.

Maybe Hanna had sensed that something happened to me when I was dancing with Alesha. In the days that followed, she asked me a few times what was going on. "Nothing," I'd tell her. Today, I realize I didn't succeed in fooling Hanna. She knew better than I did, and she must have been afraid she would lose me if she didn't give in to my desire. She must have mulled it over again and again because when we finally did it, or more precisely, when we finally tried to do it, she went about it in such a strangely determined and almost relaxed manner that it seemed as if she had thought it through a hundred times.

Hanna's parents were away. They flew to the Gulf of Mexico for occasional long weekends. In Galveston, Hanna's grandparents on her father's side had a large boat—a yacht. Up until then, Hanna had always gone with them. But not this time, even though her grandparents were celebrating their forty-second wedding anniversary. Hanna's soccer team, the Sidewinders, had a match scheduled against the Hotspurs from Tonkawa in a semifinal for the county championship. After the last practice on Friday evening, she came to the edge of the pitch, brutally motivated and incredibly sweaty. It was hot that evening, almost unbearably muggy, although the sun was already going down. I sat in the metal bleachers, my legs stretched out in front of me, my old cowboy boots dusty and my jeans were torn above the left knee.

My clothes stuck to my body. I would have preferred going down to the pond, stripping down and diving in. But Mitch had told me that morning that there was not much more left of it but a stinking quagmire that quickly would dry up if it didn't begin to rain soon.

There were tons of dead frogs and amphibians. Mitch couldn't save them all, even though, walking back and forth, and back and forth, he sometimes lugged six or seven gallons of water down to the pond and was completely exhausted afterward.

Hanna had the ball under her arm. Her T-shirt stuck to her. Her face was full of red blotches, the strands of her hair wet from sweat and from the water she had cooled herself with before Coach Bob held his pep talk. That took fifteen minutes, and I could hear it because a light wind was blowing across the field, directly toward me.

"People, think about it. Tomorrow, we have a chance to take a giant step closer to the championship. What we have achieved up until now have been small steps. The victory against the Hornets from Parker, a small step. Kicking the ass of the Palo Duro Blue Devils, another small step. Then the match against the Buckeye Bison's, only half a step because we weren't ready to give our best. Do you remember? One goal to nil at halftime. Then, the penalty that wasn't one. And finally, the equalizer. I don't want to remind you of that game because I know how the draw hurt and still hurts now. I only want to say to you what I have said a hundred times before because it simply is the truth: To win a game against a good team doesn't just require soccer skills, which you all have. It requires determination! It requires a heart!"

A Heart. With that one last word, Coach Bob had them all right where he wanted them. He gave them everything they needed to win the game the next day against the Hotspurs, as well as what they would have needed to turn around the game against Buckeye at the last minute.

For a full minute, nobody spoke. It seemed nobody even took a breath.

"I know you, guys," coach Bob then said. I know that nobody will give up tomorrow before this match is in the bag. No matter how much pain, no matter how heavy your legs will get, no matter what it will look like inside your head, nobody is going to give up. Each of you is going fight until you collapse. That's what I want to see. I want to see you fight on when you think you don't have the strength for it. You have the strength because it doesn't come from just anywhere; it comes from within your heart. Tomorrow, there will be no reason for any of you to give up unless you can't go on anymore and die miserably on the pitch. But before that happens, you'll puke. That is the safety valve built into every one of you. Everybody pukes before they croak. Remember this, when you think you cannot go on any longer. I'll pull you out only then, just before you croak. Is that clear?"

They nodded and said, "Yes, Coach," and Hanna raised her fist and shouted, "We'll beat the Hotspurs! And then we'll take the title! We're the Sidewinders! We know we can beat anybody!"

"And why do we know that?"

"Because we have the heart!"

"And because we'll fight until we collapse and puke!"

I don't know how Coach Bob was able to turn Hanna into a small, rock-hard monster ready to kick the Hotspur's goalkeeper in the knee with her studs. Exactly that was what happened the next day.

But now, as she came to me with her sports bag and her Sidewinder eyes, it was clear that she was ready to give her life for Coach Bob and the team.

I didn't like him — Coach Bob, I mean. I didn't like the way he treated the girls. As if they were boys. But that wasn't what they were. Once, I heard him say that his girls were better than boys because they didn't have peckers. He said that in the Lone Star Café, and I heard it only because I went in there with Wayne to get a Coke. Wayne was in the restroom, and I didn't have anything else to do but listen to the men at the table next to the window. Without blinking an eye, Coach Bob told them that the boys had too many problems because their peckers got in the way of their thinking. Real funny, huh. And Rusty Farley, who ran a heating and air conditioning repair shop with his twin brother, Chris, said that women had other problems, especially when they got their period. He didn't say period, but "Red Zora," or something like that, but Coach Bob said that was not so bad since there were tampons, but he was afraid that all of them would get fat asses at some stage during their puberty because that was part of a girl's nature. And Chris said that his woman had an ass like the Budweiser horses that pulled the beer wagon, and Rusty Farley almost laughed himself sick imagining it. Of course, I never told Hanna about what I had overheard, because Hanna is one of those people who get awful depressed when someone makes them doubt the goodness in people. Also, there was really no reason to talk badly about Coach Bob Kushner, because he treated the girls decently and he was always there for them. But I still didn't like him.

That Friday evening, after practice, I went with Hanna a little way down the path that led to the Brewster Pond. And there we lay down on the grass and stared up at the evening sky, which was already full of twinkling lights. I couldn't stop myself from becoming aroused. It had been happening these days quickly. I only had to imagine how it would be if Alesha were lying naked next to me. That was all it took. I got so hard that it was like having a buffalo horn in my pants, and I couldn't think of anything else, even when I tried as hard as I could to think of something else. I imagined how I would put my hand between her legs and how she would open her legs and look at me with this strange look because she knew it was the first time for me. And in my fantasy, she can't predict what's coming next, but it doesn't matter; whatever it is, she wants it.

Of course, I had never told Hanna anything about my Alesha dreams. She only knew that Alesha was with my father. But in Winstel, it was evident to everyone, including Hanna, that one day Jim Fletcher would take off again and leave Alesha in the lurch.

So, Hanna and I were lying there, and the mosquitoes were dancing around us making a hellishly unpleasant high-pitched buzzing noise. And I thought that it was finally going to happen, and I wanted to start taking off her blouse and sports bra to stroke her breasts, but she said she didn't want to because she was all sweaty. She also said we could go to her house as soon as it got a bit darker. I didn't want to do that, and I told her so, but she said that the mosquitoes were terrible, and she began to scratch herself. I believe it was more her nerves than the mosquitoes. Anyone who has lived in Winstel for more than a year got used to the mosquitoes and didn't even notice their bite.

While my hands wandered over her body, I began to ache. Of course, Hanna noticed what had been growing in my pants. She began to nibble on my ear while I pushed my hand into her soccer shorts. I felt the goose pimples on her butt cheeks, and my fingers suddenly touched hair, and it was strange how wiry it felt when she was so proud of her silky soft hair. At this moment, I didn't think of Alesha. Honestly, I only thought about doing everything right but that I didn't have a rubber with me and that I'd have to be hellishly careful so that she didn't suddenly become pregnant.

Right on cue, she whispered, "I like you, Brad, and sometimes I think about sleeping with you, but I believe doing it tonight would be premature."

Premature. Hanna said that as my fingers had almost got to the place where they'd already been a hundred times in my imagination, but now she pressed her legs together.

"Premature?" I coughed. "How long do you want to wait? Until it's night or until we're both old and gray?"

She laughed and began to pull on my arm. I took my hand out of her soccer shorts and turned over to the other side. She didn't need to see my erection if she didn't want to do it. And so we were lying there, and I didn't move. I waited for her to move an arm or a leg so that I could move, too, but she didn't. After a while, though, I felt her press herself up against me. I felt her breasts on my back, and her breath on my neck and her hand slid across and down my side and over my pants. And then she did something that she'd never done before. She began to unbutton my jeans. It was completely dark now. Clouds of mosquitoes met here at the pond for an open-air concert. And I was ready. I was only waiting for something to happen when she suddenly said, her voice trembling like never before, that I should go home with her and that we should cool off in the swimming pool.

That cracked me up. I would never have expected her to take the initiative, unbuttoning my pants with one hand, while babbling on about going swimming. It wasn't right. Hanna had her hand in my pants, held my hard-on between her fingers like a club, and talked about cooling off in her father's damn pool.

All the thoughts that swirled through my head weren't thoughts anymore, but a terrible mess in which, of course, Alesha appeared. But it was Hanna who was pressing against me from behind, and I couldn't believe it when she began jerking me off. Well, I had no idea at all what was going on. She probably didn't know herself what she was doing because she had never done it before and didn't want to do such a thing in the first place. To press her body against me and to take my prick into her hand, as if it were the most natural thing in the world to do.

All I could think was that this wasn't possible, and then it was all over way too soon. Like a volcanic eruption. It lasted only a few seconds at the most until the thing in her hand exploded. I felt it clearly, and it didn't start down there. It started in my head, where everything suddenly cramped up. The blood clogged my arteries. It was as if someone blew hot air through me at full power. Then, I felt that I could no longer hold it back, and the stuff forced itself from me, past my belly and onto the dry grass. And she didn't let go. She held onto it until she realized that we did it. As soon as it was over, I realized I'd done something crazy. I believe she knew it too. She let go and ran away. I didn't know what made her leave, but when I got up and struggled to button up my jeans, she was gone.

I called her, but she didn't answer. I looked around for a while until I finally found her. She was crouching behind one of the cottonwood trees on the other side of the pond and was crying. I sat next to her, and she sobbed that she hadn't wanted that.

"We screwed up," I said. "It was stupid."

She cried next to me, and I mean she simply cried her eyes out.

"It'd be better if we forgot this, Hanna," I said to her.

"You never took my thing in your hand."

"You're — your thing?" she sobbed. "Oh, dear God — "

I put an arm around her shoulders to comfort her. I felt sorry for her. Dear little Hanna. Always decent. Always good. The apple of her father's eye. Coach Bob Kushner's Hanna. And now she didn't know who she was anymore.

She leaned her head against my shoulder and wept.

I was angry with myself. Not because of what we had done, but because I felt as if I had forced Hanna to do it. At least, I had allowed it.

"It didn't happen," I said and the wind, which suddenly picked up, took the words from my lips and carried them out into the prairie, to Ambush Canyon, where you could hear voices whispering every night.

CHAPTER 11
IN THE PINK LIGHT

"Come on, I'll take you home," I said to Hanna. I helped her to her feet, and we walked up the path. Winstel was to our right, a collection of newer houses and a few old buildings made from sandstone.

Her parents' house stood on a little hill, higher than the other houses in Winstel and somewhat separate. Hanna cried the whole way back, and as we stood in front of her house, she didn't ask whether I wanted to come in.

"If I'd only gone with mom and dad, this would never have happened," she said. She seemed confused and began to talk about how happy her grandparents always were when she visited them in Galveston and how her grandfather had taught her how to gut a fish. She asked me when I would be visiting my grandmother in Memphis.

I had no desire to talk to her about it, so I told her I had to go home, and she said that was okay. We didn't kiss. We didn't even dare to look at each other.

"Well, goodbye," she said awkwardly.

"Yeah," I replied. "Goodbye."

I went home and pulled out the old shoebox. I picked up the picture I'd studied that often, every detail etched in my memory. It showed a young woman, almost a girl, sitting on a bicycle. I mean, she was standing over the bicycle, one hand on the handlebars, the other protecting her hair from the wind. She had a strange smile on her face, half happy and half distrustful as if someone had talked her into having the picture taken. On the back of it was my grandmother's name: Lilly. And a date that someone had erased. I could only make out a one and a nine.

The way Lilly looked she must have been about eighteen years old. It's not easy to determine the age of people photographed almost half a century ago.

Every time I picked up this photo, I studied it for a long time. Lilly was a graceful and pretty young woman, with blonde hair that had been tossed about by the wind from riding the bicycle. The expression in her eyes was curious, but also skeptical.

Another photo showed her sitting on a bench somewhere, leaning against a clapboard wall. Next to her sat a dark-skinned, spindly man wearing a hat. Nothing of his face could be seen but the whites of his eyes and his teeth. The man wore a suit and a white shirt and tie. He was sitting beside Lilly, but there was a gap between them, so they didn't touch. Lilly had her hands in her lap and sat straight as a board. The man was also sitting straight and held a guitar on his knees with his right hand. His left hand was out of focus because he must have had just moved it, putting a cigarette in his mouth or taking it out. I often looked at this photo, too, but it didn't take me long to discover a veil of smoke in front of the timber wall that one could only see by looking at the photo through a magnifying glass. And I had done that several times. On the back of the photo, somebody had written the letters JB. Nothing else. But I believe that once there had been something else on the back. It had been rubbed out with an eraser. Even with a magnifying glass, I could not recognize what had been there. Maybe it was a year or the name of a town. I kept these two photos and was determined to show them to Lilly at some point.

I said so to my mother.

She laughed.

"Lilly doesn't want to think about this old story anymore, Brad. It's plagued her long enough."

In the days that followed, I wrote Lilly a letter telling her that I would be visiting Memphis. Apart from that, I couldn't concentrate on anything. What had happened with Hanna was driving me crazy. For a few weeks, we couldn't look each other in the eye. What on earth had we done? I even considered discussing it with someone. With Wayne perhaps, or with Reverend Birch, our Baptist Minister. I didn't, though. Instead, it became more evident, during the restless nights that followed, that only Alesha could save me. I didn't know how, but it was no surprise that I hit on the crazy idea of driving to Dickens with Jesse Walker's pickup to visit Alesha. I knew she'd rented a room at the Starlight Motel. I asked Jesse if he'd lend me his pickup. He grinned, told me not to get caught by the cops, and handed me the keys. I went home first, showered, rubbed pomade into my hair, put on my best shirt, and told only Wayne that I'd be going to Dickens to visit Alesha.

His eyes lit up. "You're a crazy dog, Brad," he said. "Like your father."

91

"Not like him," I contradicted, but somehow it made me proud he thought that.

I traveled on the ramrod-straight highway to Dickens, turned into the parking lot of the Starlight Motel, and asked in the lobby for Alesha Prosser's room. The man sized me up from head to foot.

"Do I know you?"

"I've never been here before."

"And who are you?"

"Steve Prosser," I said. "Alesha's brother."

"Oh, I didn't know she had a brother. But the pickup out there—isn't that Walker's truck? Jesse Walker, the old cowhand? Winstel, I guess he lives?"

"That's right," I said, holding his gaze with a steady eye.

He didn't ask any more questions; he just told me Alesha's room number. My hands were blocks of ice as I was walking down the long corridor, past the other rooms and their windows, some dark, others with light shimmering through the curtains. Number eighteen. I stopped in front of it. My courage had almost left me, and I was ready to turn around and run away. But then I knocked, and she opened the door and stood there in her transparent nightgown, the crazy pink light behind her. She didn't say a word, just let me come in.

That's how it happened. Alesha saved me. It didn't matter that she only wanted to take revenge on my father. Of course, she didn't tell me that, but I wouldn't have cared. I had come because I needed her.

And, as she had taught me to dance at Lilly's birthday

party, she led me out of my dreams back into reality, where I had felt completely lost before.

As I drove back to Winstel, I knew I got restored to what I'd been before Hanna, and I did what we did. I was Old Bradley Fletcher again. Only, I didn't want to let myself that easily be thrown off the tracks anymore. Not by anyone.

CHAPTER 12
BEALE STREET BLUES

Sara Carter's used bookstore was located on South Lauderdale Street, at the intersection of Beale Street. When I entered, a small bell rang above the door, but I was unable to see whether there was anyone in the shop. The room was crammed with books. It seemed one could hardly turn around without knocking over a bookshelf, and one collapsing shelf would have knocked over all the other shelves crisscrossing the store. A literary domino effect.

I didn't dare move. I stood between two bookshelves that sagged under the weight of centuries of agony, wisdom, and dreams. One minute went by, then another. The air and the silence in the shop made me drowsy. I almost fell asleep standing there, but then got startled by the sound of a toilet getting flushed somewhere. First, a waterfall, and then a roar, as if a gorge had opened up to swallow the entire bookshop, and then, finally, the usual noise of draining water. Nothing else. I carefully proceeded between the shelves until I got to an old writing desk surrounded by mountains of books. A gray cat was lying among the mess and observing me furtively with her pale yellow eyes. I started to get goosebumps and wanted to turn around and leave, when, behind the desk, a dark red velvet curtain opened, and a small creature appeared. At first, I mistook it for a giant crow. After a second look, I saw that it was not a bird, but an old woman whose back was stooped with age as if she had been carrying the weight of all the books ever written on her shoulders for decades.

Two dark eyes looked at me over the rim of a pair of reading glasses.

"Do you have a problem, boy?" It was a voice that would have suited a crow just as well.

"Me? Not at all."

She nodded.

"Fine. But I do have a problem. Once again, the toilet isn't working. The water tank, I mean. And I cannot get up there, not even on tiptoes. Would you give me a hand, young man?"

I shrugged, and the woman opened the curtain and a small door behind it. The bathroom was so tiny that I wondered how on earth one could wipe one's ass without being a contortionist. The water tank located on the wall above the toilet bowl lacked a lid. I got up on the toilet seat and, following the old woman's croaking instructions, lifted the rusted chain stuck between the discharge outlet and the downpipe. Water was again flowing into the tank and through the pipe into the toilet bowl, which looked like it was made from the ivory of a yellow-brown elephant tooth.

"Thanks. Thanks a lot," said the woman. "You know, I should have this thing repaired someday, but then again, I always think that I'll stop taking care of this fine bookstore soon anyway and then the big bulldozers will come and raze everything to the ground."

"The books must be rescued," I replied with conviction because I couldn't think of anything else to say. But the woman probably didn't hear me, as she sat down behind the desk, adjusted her glasses, and started to pet the cat. Then, she looked up at me.

"I haven't seen one like you in here for ages. Sometimes, students come here looking for specific things, but young men like you rarely come in here. The last one who did was carrying a gun. Just wanted the dough. He positioned himself right in front of me just like that and said, 'Hand over the dough, Granny!' I smacked him in the face, and he just ran off. Later, I felt sorry for him. He looked pretty down and out, the little guy. He was just a kid. But the cops said I did it all wrong. Always hand over the money straight away, they said, because these little punks have no respect, for anything. Not for life, and most certainly not for somebody else's property. They shoot without thinking, no matter if there's ten dollars or twenty-five cents on the cash register."

"I'm here because a cop told me that Sara Carter knows what happened here some fifty years ago. Before the war."

"Thirty-five, thirty-seven. The drought years? Mr. Steinbeck wrote an excellent novel about that. The Grapes of Wrath."

"Haven't read that one yet."

"Then it's about time you did," she said sternly. "It's over there, on the shelf — the paperback edition. Not in the best condition. You can have it for free."

"Thanks."

"And what is it you want to know from me?"

"Everything."

"Then you're in the wrong place. I know a lot, not everything. If you're looking for somebody who knows everything, you should try at the dry cleaner's next door. A smart-ass little girl works there. Her name is Gina, and she talks as if she knows it all."

"Everything that happened here back then," I corrected myself.

"Here?" She turned her head to one side as if she could get a better look at me if she looked at me with only one eye.

"Did you know JB?"

"JB?" This woman looked right through me, studying my insides. I felt like a fish that had just been slit open and whose guts were being pushed out by the fisherman's thumb. "What do you want to know about JB?"

"What happened when he shot the man?"

"How come you know about that?"

"I've heard about it."

"And why do you want to know?"

"My grandmother told me about it."

"Your grandmother?"

"Yes."

"And who is she?"

"My grandmother."

She laughed. "You're quite a stubborn young fellow, aren't you? What's your name?"

"Brad."

"I'm Sara Carter," she said. "Why don't you ask your granny, if she told you about it?"

"I will ask her, at some point."

"Or ask Gina, next door. Talking to her you get to think that she was on this planet two or three times over."

She scratched the cat behind the ear. She was no longer looking at me. In fact, I could tell that part of her wasn't even there with me anymore. Her eyes had turned inward so that she was better able to see what was happening inside her head. I just stood there getting scared. Scared that something horrible would happen to her; that she'd suffer a stroke or something right in front of me. Or the cat would suddenly jump at me and turn into a full-grown panther during the leap. The store felt spooky, and I began to wish I had never come here.

"Those weren't good times, back then," she started. "Not like in the twenties, when this street attracted the best. They came from everywhere, the big cats of the time. I'll tell you just a few names, kid, but these names ring in my ears like music. William Bailey…" She paused as if she were listening to the ring of the name as if it were a magic melody, forcing its way into her ears over the air. She softly continued her list. "Johnny Dunn, George Duff, the cornet player of the Georgia Minstrels, Furry Jackson, Sleepy John Estes, Willie Weldon, and Noah Lewis. They were all young then. They all had big dreams. To take their music out into the world, to Chicago and New York, to Paris, Berlin, and London. Some of them were successful, but there were some who fell by the wayside. Before the war, Beale Street was merciless. It would destroy those who weren't careful. And one of those was JB Swift."

"What happened?"

"He had everything he ever wanted. He had more talent than all the others. More luck. And friends in all the right places. Women following him wherever he went, adoring him, wanting to be with him, to have his baby. The Legend, that's what they called him. He was producing his first records. His song "Bayou Baby" was played on the radio; even made it into the charts. JB had been to New York and Chicago. Then he returned to the street that had made him big. Beale Street. But everything here had changed in the years just before the war. The old ones had moved away, and riff-raff had taken over. They all wanted to make a quick buck. Nobody stuck to the old rules anymore. The dance halls turned into bars, where people gambled. The place was crawling with mobsters and pimps, and their fancy women and sleazy girls. Those days weren't fun; let me tell you, not at all like the good old times. Nothing was the way it used to be anymore."

"What happened to JB?"

"What happened to JB? I'll tell you what happened to JB. He made a mistake, boy. He made the terrible mistake of falling in love with a white girl. Many of the others would have liked to have made the same mistake, but JB was the one who wouldn't let himself to be held back by anyone or anything. There were plenty of warning signs. I still remember. His friends warned him. He laughed at them. He thought he was untouchable. Invincible. He made this girl, a delicate, pretty little thing from the suburbs, his girlfriend. No idea where he picked her up.

I think he had met her for the first time somewhere else. But then, she came to the Royal Blue with a scoundrel named Crazy Legs. A tap-dancer. Pretty slippery type rumored to have connections to the mob and the police. No idea who he was or where he came from. Suddenly, he turned up like a ghost, and when everything was over, he was gone. JB supposedly took the girl from him. Anyway, something was gnawing at Crazy Legs like rats' teeth. It destroyed him. Most likely, he didn't think about anything else other than how to pay JB back for that. At some point, he came up with the idea to have a word with the girl's father. That was the beginning of the end. I believe JB got warned several times, but he didn't listen to anybody. I think he loved the girl insanely. What I mean by that is, he could have had them all, the cream of the crop, but he chose this cute little white girl. And he adored her. Nobody dared mention his or her color, or he would go crazy. Later, I learned that he had waited an entire year to meet her again, without touching any of the other women. And then, it happened the way it had to happen. Nobody knows what exactly did happen, and for a time, all sorts of rumors went around. They said that the girl's father had called JB and even met up with him. According to another story, he had attempted to send the girl to another college, in Boston or wherever wealthy people sent their children. It was also later said that JB had threatened the girl's father with taking her to New York and marrying her there. And that must have been when the father blew his top. Talk of the street had it that her daddy was a big shot well connected to high-ranking civil servants in the city. One of his buddies was the Chief of Police. One night, when the girl was in the Royal Blue, the cops made a raid. They arrested JB. They took the girl and handed her over to her father. I don't know what the cops did to JB, but when they set him free, he was a different person. Only, nobody knew at the time because he didn't let on. On the outside, he was still the old JB we all knew and many adored, though we all knew he had given his heart to the white girl. Lilly was her name, I believe. Lilly. And when he was with her, he laughed. He was happy. Nobody knew the anger was smoldering inside of him. He was very good at hiding all that. I believe he hadn't even told her who had been responsible for the raid and his arrest. Later, I learned he had bought a revolver from Perkins."

"What for?"

"What does one buy a revolver for, young man?"

"To kill somebody."

"It's possible he wanted to do that. But who? Certainly not her father. I think he bought the revolver for another reason — to protect himself."

"From whom?"

"I think he knew who was out to destroy his luck. Crazy Legs. Eventually, rumor had it that the girl's father gave Crazy Legs money to teach JB a lesson. One last warning. But JB kept his eyes open. In the Royal Blue, they were never able to get close to him, as friends always surrounded him. They had to catch him out somewhere else, but he was with the girl most of the time. They probably spied on him for many weeks before they were ready to go through with it and collect their blood money. They were waiting for him and the girl in front of Frank's Café. I was inside the café at the time. I saw them both sitting at their small round table, and they were holding hands and talking to each other and laughing. I thought it would be a sin to destroy such happiness, though I was jealous, of course. I hated the girl who had stolen one of our best men. I was still in the café when JB asked for the check. Then they left, and you know what happened outside, right?"

"I've only heard that they tore the girl away from him and beat him up. With a baseball bat."

"Yes. I heard the screaming and the cursing, and when I rushed to the window, JB was already lying on the ground, and the men ran away, and then, all of a sudden, he had the revolver in his hand and fired a shot. One of the men, the one with the baseball bat, fell; at first, I thought he had stumbled and would get up again and run on, but he didn't get up. When I saw the blood, a pool of blood beneath him, I ran outside, and JB stood there staring at the revolver in his hand as if he had never seen it before. At that second, he realized he had lost everything, and there was nothing he could do to undo what had happened. He was unable to save anything, not even himself. He let the cops arrest him without resisting, and later, they took him to court, and he never said a single word during the entire trial. Not a word."

"He was convicted."

"For premeditated murder. The prosecuting attorneys demanded the death penalty, but the judge exercised clemency and sentenced JB to life in prison. If there's injustice in this world, then it was that verdict. Everybody here in the street knew it. It wasn't premeditated murder. If it was murder at all, it was a 'murder committed in the heat of passion,' or something like that. For many, it was nothing more than self-defense, but the bullet hit the man in the back and, of course, even the best attorney in the world couldn't paint that as self-defense. Less so in the case of a black man who shot down a white guy. The other way round, it would have been possible, but not in this case. The other way round doesn't exist, murder of a black man. In any case, it didn't live at the time. Do you understand?"

"I get it," I mumbled, even though I was kind of confused and wanted to bring order to my thoughts.

"Some old folks told me that JB died in prison, some years ago. In any case, people never saw him back here and never heard any more about him, other than that he had died."

The woman got up from the chair and came around the desk, between the towers of books. She grabbed my arm. "You don't want to believe that he's dead, right?"

"Maybe he's dead; maybe he isn't. I'll find out."

"And then?"

"I'll search for him. And if he has died, I'll find his grave."

She nodded, as if she hadn't expected anything else from me, and got up with a sigh and hobbled past me, her shoulders hunched as if she were about to turn into a crippled crow for real. She stopped at one of the shelves and fished for a thin book among other books. It was bound in black linen and looked well-thumbed. Sara Carter hobbled back to the desk and sat down again. Without a word, she opened the book and flipped through the pages. I stood there and didn't know whether to stay or leave. After about two minutes, she stopped and looked at a particular page.

"There," she said. "This may be of interest to you." She pushed the book toward me. The cat clawed at it but didn't get a hold of it. On the page she had opened to was a photo. In black and white. It showed a man in a bright suit, leaning against a bar. He wasn't wearing a hat. His face was dark, the light in the bar poor. Despite that, I realized it was not JB. He was smaller and slimmer. Underneath the photo, it said that this man was Bukka "Crazy Legs" Harris, at the bar of the newly opened Crazy Legs Dance Club in Baton Rouge.

I tried to see into the man's eyes, but he closed them grinning into the camera with his eyes shut as if he had anticipated the flash.

"What do you see?" Sue Carter asked.

"Someone who's afraid of the light," I said.

"A little runt," she said. "I never liked him. He had something mean to him. He always knew everything about everybody, without actually knowing anything. He was cunning too. Always had sticky hands. I can remember his hands well because I slept with him two or three times."

She took the book in her bony hands and looked at the picture.

"You should take a close look at the guitar on the wall behind the bar, kid. I noticed the guitar at once when I first saw the photo."

She pushed the book over to me again. There were several guitars on the wall behind the bar Crazy Legs was leaning against.

"Which one?" I asked.

She pointed to it. "That was JB's guitar. He called it The Ham. That's the way he was. Others gave their guitars the name of their lover, but JB called it his ham."

I studied the guitar but didn't notice anything special about it.

"How do you know it's JB's guitar?"

"I know because I know the guitar very well. I saw it in his hands often enough. At the back, when you turn it around, it says who it belongs to. JB is written on it."

"And how come Crazy Legs came to own it?"

She shrugged. "No idea. But a few weeks after the sentencing, this runt left Memphis. Nobody knew where he went. One year later, he opened the dance club in Baton Rouge, and JB's guitar was the showpiece of his small collection of guitars of famous blues musicians."

"Is Crazy Legs still alive?"

"I don't know. I only know the dance club doesn't exist anymore. There's a bank where it used to be now." She tapped the book with her finger. "This has been on the shelf for years. If you want it, you can have it."

"Thanks," I said and wanted to take the book from the table, but she put a hand on top of mine and left it there.

"You're welcome," she said. "Tell me, what's your

grand-mother's name?"

"Lilly."

I pulled my hand away, took the book from the table, turned around and wanted to leave.

"Don't forget to take Steinbeck's book!" she shouted after me. "The Grapes of Wrath."

I searched for the book, found it on one of the overloaded shelves, and put it into my pocket. Then I left the bookshop. Once outside, I had to take a deep breath. It was afternoon, the sun was shining, and I made my way to the retirement home.

CHAPTER 13
FAMILY HONOR

They were sitting at the same table, near the small lobby, drinking coffee and eating cake. Just like last time, when I was nine and came here with my father. Nothing had changed, except the people sitting there. The people I had seen long ago had made room for others. They were secretly observing each other like four vultures with wrinkly necks. Nobody spoke. Four men, no women. I thought Sara Carter would have gotten along well with them. They were eating their cake, and one of them, a pale man with nearly translucent skin and red-rimmed eyes, dozed off. The one in the wheelchair was waiting for just that and stole a piece of cake from his plate. The third one also grabbed a bit but used his fingers doing so, and after he had swallowed it, he meticulously licked them clean.

"This is disgusting," said the one in the wheelchair.

"What?" the other man said.

"How you're licking your fingers. It makes me sick watching you."

A woman, who was sitting at the window, asked for the nurse.

"She's peed in her pants again," said the finger licker. "I can smell it." He slowly turned his chair until the woman was in view. The woman was impatiently tapping her walking stick on the ground and calling for the nurse louder.

"Sue, let them put diapers on you," he shouted.

The myna bird said something I couldn't make out. The door of the elevator opened, and I almost collided with Nurse Rhonda.

"Hello, Brad. Lilly isn't feeling very well this afternoon. She wanted me to draw the curtains for her."

"Is she awake?"

"I think so. She's lying on her bed, but I believe, in her thoughts, she's somewhere else. I asked her, but she wouldn't give me an answer. Sometimes, I think she no longer wants to hear or see anything."

I got on the elevator. The room was dark. Lilly was lying on the bed with her eyes open. She didn't hear me come in. Only when I cleared my throat did she turn her head to look at me. She looked tired. Her hair was uncombed.

"I've been waiting for you for a long time, Bradley," she said, though it had only been three hours since I brought her back to the home after the meal at McDonald's.

"We had lunch together," I said.

"That was yesterday," she contradicted me. I realized it was pointless to correct her.

I helped her sit up. I took one of the cushions and stuffed it behind her back.

"The sun is shining," I said. "If you don't mind, I'll open the curtains."

She didn't mind. When I opened the curtains and the window, the sun was shining into the room. Its light seemed to recharge her. I saw it in her eyes when the ghosts of her life woke up.

"I shouldn't have eaten last night. It upset my stomach.

We had chicken and broccoli."

"Maybe it was the Big Mac we had for lunch," I said, poking fun at her.

"Certainly not," she answered.

She remembered where we'd been for lunch, but she'd already forgotten how convinced she was just a moment ago that we hadn't yet seen each other that day.

"Nurse Lisa also suggested it was the Big Mac, but I don't think so. The other people here can't digest a Big Mac anymore, but I've never gotten sick from a Big Mac. More likely from the stuff they serve us here."

I promised to have another Big Mac with her before I left for home, with fries and a big Coke and with lots of ketchup.

"Bradley, I want to tell you something significant," Lilly said as I sat down on the windowsill, admiring how quickly she could read my thoughts. I was just about to ask her how it all happened that day, the day JB killed a man. And I wanted to tell her that I had been to Beale Street in the morning, at the intersection with South Lauderdale, where once there had been the billiard hall and Frank's Café. And that I had met Sara Carter in her bookshop after lunch to find out what happened that day.

Lilly started to talk about the day her father intercepted her at the university, as she was on her way to class. He stepped out of the shade of a tree and straight into her path. He grabbed her by the upper arm so hard that all her books fell to the ground. A boy named Billy Carmichel, who was heading to the same class, asked whether something was wrong.

"Everything is just fine," Lilly's father snapped. "I'm her father!"

"You're hurting me," Lilly said, but he didn't let go of her. In fact, his grip tightened.

"I've just found out what you're up to, Lilly!" he hissed. "I know where you're hanging about, and with whom. You know that I cannot tolerate it. Just think of your mother and the whole family. You'll have to make up your mind, Lilly. It could be your only chance."

"I don't understand what you mean," Lilly had said. "Please, let go of my arm."

"Come with me to the car."

He dragged her with him, although she told him that her class was due to start in a few minutes. He considered school to be of secondary importance. All that mattered now was the family's honor.

"We drove out of town in his new station wagon," Lilly said, carefully searching for the right words, probably because that day determined everything that came after. "He was very proud of his station wagon. His first new car. It was green, with wooden panels on the sides. When he bought it, he called me at the dormitory. 'I want to show you our new car,' he said, and then he came over, with mom in the passenger seat. She was wearing a little straw hat and her Sunday dress. We drove all over town and over the Mississippi bridge to Beulah, halfway down to Little Rock, Arkansas, and he wound the side window down so that in the back seat, the air blew my hair around my face, and he told us all about the new engine and everything he had learned from the car salesman. Mom and I had no clue about engine size or horsepower. But this time, when he forced me to go with him, he went silent as soon as we sat in the car.

"We drove out of town, and I had no idea where we were heading. I paid no attention to the street signs; until I noticed we were somewhere I had never been before — nothing but farmland and a few scattered houses and a telephone pole and power line by the roadside.

"Father switched on the radio. Country music. All the time, he was staring straight ahead. I watched him from the side. For the longest time, he drummed his fingers on the steering wheel then stopped. He was wearing a hat, with the brim pulled down over his forehead. I didn't know why I was suddenly afraid of him. Never before had I felt threatened by him. But now, I wished I hadn't gone with him.

"He switched off the radio and startled me. He began to talk about how beautiful this country was and how proud we should be. This country was once a wilderness, he said. Brave people had conquered it and cultivated it. For a better future. For us. My great-grandfather was the first of our family to come here. From Ohio. In a covered wagon. Shortly before the Civil War. With his wife and seven children. He fought in the Civil War for the South. For the rights of free people. In the battle of Antietam, he gave his left leg for it. And toward the end of the war, near Appomattox, he gave his oldest son, who wasn't even thirteen. And then, after the war, in the seventies, during a series of cholera and yellow fever epidemics, he fell ill, as thousands of other people did. In Memphis alone, five thousand were said to have died, and over 25,000 fled the epidemic. But my great-grandmother held out with her children, losing three of them in the process. She fell ill, but by a miracle, she managed to stay alive.

"I knew all that. It wasn't the first time my father had told me about it. As a child, he had often heard about those days, and I remember that, on several occasions, we visited the field where many of the victims were buried.

"To be honest, my father's talk was giving me the creeps. Because he talked as if the end of the world were near, with a monotonous and insistent voice. At some point, I thought he'd stop, and some cherubs with trumpets would descend from the flaming sky, and the earth would open and all the dead people from that time would rise from their graves and surround us."

Lilly smiled to herself while she said this, but a moment later, her eyes turned more serious and hard, in a way I'd never seen before.

"Somewhere out there, where there were no houses or anything else for that matter, he stopped at the side of the road and switched off the engine.

"'This cemetery doesn't exist anymore,' my father said, 'but your great-grandfather's heritage does, and you should not mess with it.'

"Finally, he'd gotten to the point: in our family, nobody went out with a Negro. Not that he had anything against Negros. On the contrary, he had taught the class in schools for Negros, but there were rules and laws of decency in our family, which could never be broken. Never! One of those laws was that a woman from our family could never go out with a Negro.

"The whole time he was talking, he didn't look at me once. Rather than looking at him, I stared down at my hands in my lap.

"Suddenly, he turned his head. 'You contravened that law, Lilly! You lied to your parents. Instead of working, you have been going out with a man to whom the honor of our family means nothing. You have broken my trust and that of your mother, and you have brought shame upon yourself. You understand that I have to protect our family from further harm. Therefore, I'm asking you now whether you've slept with that man.'

"I didn't move and remained silent. Then, in a voice so low I could barely understand the words, he asked me to look at him. I lifted my head and looked at him. At that very moment, I knew I was prepared to break away from him. He was my father. That was a fact. I appreciated what he had done for me, but I didn't want to let him destroy my happiness and my future. He had no right to do so. Nor did my mother. I believe he grasped, in that same instant he realized he didn't have power over me anymore. Even before I said a word, he understood as much, because my eyes told him.

"'I love him,' I replied. 'You will not change that.'

"Then he hit me. Just the once. He hit me in the face with the back of his hand. I couldn't believe it. Never before had he hit me. I was bleeding from my eyebrow.

"I looked at him and saw the fear in his eyes, and

though he was screaming, I could hardly hear him.

"'Think about your mother! She's ill! She worries about you!'

"'I can't do what you ask me to,' I replied. I felt each word sinking deep into him, hurting him bad. I saw it on his face. It was as if he was petrified. An impenetrable mask with eyes full of hatred. Not hatred toward me. He wasn't capable of that. It was hatred toward the man who, in his opinion, was destroying the family, hatred toward JB.

"'Then do it for your own sake, Lilly! Do it for yourself! You're about to ruin your life.'

"'I don't think so.'

"'Because he's blinded you, Lilly! You believe you're happy, but in your inexperience, you don't know you're only going through a phase. One day, he'll leave you for another woman. A Negro woman. He'll realize that it's not right to mix two races. He'll yield to the pressure from his family and his friends, Lilly. One day, you'll be alone in the world you turned your back on. You'll be rejected by everyone, even your friends at school. No one will want to stand by you, and you'll wish you'd followed my advice when you still had a chance. You must leave him!'

"I didn't have a handkerchief on me to wipe off the blood. He offered me his, but I didn't take it.

"'You must leave him, Lilly!' he repeated.

"'And what if I won't?'

"He looked aghast that I even dared put that question to him. But he didn't think about it for long. I believe he had made up his mind long before that day, and his words were shiny as polished steel.

"'Then you're not one of us anymore, Lilly!'

"I didn't answer. Couldn't say a word. My throat felt as if it were tied up. My eyes were burning. I could have cried, but I didn't want to. I wanted to show him how severely he had disappointed me. I wanted to show him that I was prepared to go my own way. Ready to face all the consequences.

"'Think about it carefully,' he finally said. 'Leave him, or I will have to take care of him!'

"After this threat, he grabbed his car keys. Without saying another word, he drove back to the college, never turning on the radio.

"He stopped where he had exactly parked before. He stopped without saying a word, opened the door, and I got out. I almost fell, because my legs were shaking. I didn't have any strength left. I walked down the street, and once he had driven off, and I was sure he wouldn't see me, I sat on a bench and cried. I almost cried my soul out of my body, but it didn't help. I walked back to the dorm and only noticed on my way that I had forgotten my books on the bench. I walked back to get them, while at the same time looking out for the green station wagon, in my desperation, wishing it would reappear. But I didn't spot it anywhere."

Lilly stopped talking. I saw that she had tears in her eyes. I took one of her handkerchiefs from a drawer in the night table and handed it to her. She thanked me and wiped her eyes. Then she laughed. It was a laugh that had risen from crying. And she took my hand.

"I wasn't feeling well for a while," she said. "I was struck by a mysterious illness. It's called shingles. It's a nervous disease you get when, deep in your soul, you're unhappy. I had the decision to make. For JB or my family. To keep JB, I had to give up something I loved above all else. My parents."

"Wasn't there anyone who could have spoken to your father?" I objected.

"My father was a man who stuck to his principles. Our family's honor meant the world to him. He was proud of our ancestors, and, up to then, he also had been proud of me. I believe it was the hatred that destroyed him. He hated JB so much that he could have killed him."

"He didn't do that," I said.

"Not with his own hands," answered Lilly. "But he turned his threats into reality and didn't rest until he had destroyed JB."

She grew silent while looking out the window. The sun was low. Fair weather clouds were drifting in the sky. We could hear voices from the garden. A robin was sitting on a tree branch, looking at us.

"Yes, he destroyed JB and with him my happiness," she said, and it sounded as if she had said enough for now.

"It happened that day when JB shot a man in front of Frank's Café," I blurted out.

She looked at me.

"How do you know about that?"

"I was there today."

"You were there?"

"At Beale Street, right there, where it happened. And then I went to see Sara Carter in the bookshop. She told me what happened. She was there, in Frank's Café. She saw everything."

Lilly closed her eyes, trying to remember Sara Carter. Her hands rested on the blanket, her fingers fidgeting with the handkerchief. Several minutes went by before she opened her eyes again and looked at me.

"Then you know what happened?"

I nodded.

"Everyone thought they knew what happened. There was only one thing nobody knew. Nobody knew I was pregnant. Not even JB knew. And he never learned about it. I didn't even tell him during the trial. I didn't want to make it worse for him. I knew he'd be convicted. At first, I feared they'd sentence him to death, but they spared him that. Life in prison was what he had to deal with. For him it was hell, and it was my father who had put him there. I don't know if JB rather would have died. He never spoke to me again. Not a word. He only talked to his attorney, nobody else. And in the end, after the sentencing, when the judge asked him if he had anything else to say, he looked at me. 'It was like a dream,' was the only thing he said. I broke down. It was his friends who held me and helped me up. Later, my father wanted to see me, but I wasn't in Memphis any longer. I fled. I went to California by bus. There, I tried to make a new beginning, with all the others who had fled the drought. That's where I gave birth to your father."

She ended her story with the birth of my father. I could see that she didn't want to say anymore. She closed her eyes, and I compared her face to the one I knew from the black and white photograph.

"Are you sure he died?" I asked after a short silence.

She didn't move. She lay there as if she had fallen into a deep sleep.

"I'll look for him, Grandma," I said quietly and bent over her to kiss her softly on the mouth. To this day, I still don't understand what made me kiss her, but I kissed her as if I wanted to make a vow. When I stood up straight again, she smiled, without opening her eyes.

"I'll find him, Grandma," I said and left the room.

CHAPTER 14
WINSTEL BLUES

I know quite a few things about myself now that I didn't know then. I know that my life would have turned out differently if I hadn't made up my mind to find JB. Apart from that, I now understand that I never stood a real chance of becoming a writer. The main reason is the fact that we are living here in Winstel and that nothing ever happens in Winstel. There is hardly anything worth writing about here. In other words, Winstel is not a birthplace for writers except if you are qualified to write about nothingness. In Winstel, babies are born who turn into farmers, cowboys, or salespeople in Allister Bean's hardware store, where you can also buy CDs, ghetto blasters, CD players, and television sets. Babies who see the light of day in Winstel turn into honest folks with decent jobs and decent dreams, except Sheila Roberts, perhaps. I know that once in a while, she allows Charley McCabe to grope her under her blouse, which mostly happens down on the edge of the pond in the Brewster Valley, where the old Brewster Farm used to be before it got hit by lightning in a dry storm and burnt down. They built the farm again a few miles away from the pond, erected the big house with a huge porch, built the corrals and the stable for the horses, and the sheds and the bunkhouse. The new place was not a farm anymore but a ranch with pastures reaching as far as to the Rimrocks.

It goes without saying that I don't know what Sheila dreams of if she dreams at all. But Charley McCabe maintains that she once told him that she dreamt of becoming his wife and bearing him at least seven children, four completely healthy boys as well as three completely healthy girls, which again proves that all things have their proper place here in Winstel.

Winstel is something like a one-horse town. Whoever happens to pass through, driving along the main street, must think that Winstel only exists thanks to a bunch of people who, on their way to somewhere else, got too tired and settled in this dreary isolation. Most of the time, nothing moves in Winstel, apart from some things that are loose and shaken about by the constant prairie wind.

"This little place is clinically dead," Wayne Bundy said one time when we were sitting on the water tower late on a summer evening, looking down onto Winstel. That is the state of affairs Winstel finds itself in most of the time. Wayne is very observant. The traffic light dangles in the wind and flashes day in, day out, above the main intersection, where Jesse Walker's old gas station, the pharmacy, the General Store and the Prairie Wind Motel are located. The pulse of Winstel - blink - blink - blink. From up there where Wayne and I were sitting, one realizes that Winstel is surrounded by nothing. Nothing but the prairie and a range of hills to the south called the Rimrocks, which sometimes is just a narrow dark band and sometimes looks like a naked woman reclining, depending on how much haze there is hanging over the prairie. Above it all, there is the boundless sky, white and empty and full of heat in the summer, blue and icy cold on winter days, when a crisp cold sweeps through the land and the pond below in the Brewster Valley is covered by such a thick layer of ice that Jesse Walker can drive in circles on it with his old pickup, until one of us gets so dizzy that it turns his stomach and he pukes out the window.

Nowadays, another thing I was pretty damn sure about was in fact that I don't want to grow old in Winstel. It's nothing against the people of Winstel. I've known them since we came here and before I even knew that my grandfather was black. Aside from the fact that nobody here knows that my grandfather was black, most people have treated me like one of them, although I've never played football or baseball, and I've always gotten a severe allergy attack every time I came near a horse.

My mother, who everybody started to call Mrs. McDelcott right after she had remarried, is white. Real white, I mean, just about as white as my teeth. She's a strawberry blonde, with pale skin and freckles and blue-green eyes. When the sun shines onto her face, she breaks out in a rash. So she slathers strong sun block wherever the sun could touch her. Mitch is more like her than I am. As far as outward appearance goes, I mean. He also played football in junior high, and whenever there's an opportunity, he hangs out at the Brewster Ranch, helps with the round-up, and shows off his riding skills on a half-wild mustang. My skin is a bit darker than his, but not as dark as my father's, who looks like a Mexican, not like a black person. It wouldn't have occurred to anybody in Winstel that we could have black ancestors, even less so once mom and dad got divorced and mom married McDelcott.

Justin T. McDelcott was an old friend of my father's, and a damn decent man, who was killed by his truck a few years back. One night, when he had a flat, not even three miles from Winstel, he jacked up the car in a half-assed way, using an old jack, to check out a broken universal joint on the drive shaft. There were no witnesses to the accident, and even the sheriff from Dickens, the county seat, came over and asked around if my stepfather had any enemies, but most everybody only had good things to say about him. Even people, who didn't know him that well, called him one of theirs and a damn decent man. The whole town of Winstel seemed to be proud of him.

Apart from that, there isn't much to say about McDelcott. He had married my mother even though she had two kids from my father. I don't know exactly how it was. It's not something I would want to write about, even if I knew what happened then. The only thing I do know is that my father ran off, and then suddenly, McDelcott was there, and he didn't ask me to call him father or dad or whatever, not once, so I always called him sir, and Mitch called him dad. That's what he still calls him, whenever we talk about him.

His death came as a shock to us all, felt primarily by mother, simply because he was a responsible family man who didn't shy away from work and always lent a hand to his neighbors when they needed help.

McDelcott got buried in the cemetery behind the

church. The grave is right next to that of Hump Douglas, who, in those days, was mayor of Winstel and owner of Winstel General Store on Highway 82, which turned into Main Street once it entered Winstel. At the time, when I was a child, not that long ago, I missed McDelcott a lot, though I never really knew him. I missed him because all the other kids in Winstel had a father and because he was kind to our mother. Although I had one, I didn't want him because he didn't want us.

There is not much to be said about my brother. He's still a kid now. When it doesn't rain in spring, and the wind dries up the valley, he fills up a bucket with water every evening and carries it to the pond, so that the last little puddle, which teems big-time with amphibians, won't dry out. I like him. Sometimes I think that I'd die for him if need be. Of course, I hope that I'll never have to make such a decision, him or me, but you never know. At least, in an emergency, I believe I'd be prepared to die for him, although I'd never tell him so. He already worries about all kinds of things; the last thing he needs is for me to bring up something about dying. He once asked me if it was his fault that McDelcott had his fatal accident. I asked him how he could think that it was his fault, and he said that mom had told him that McDelcott died with a photograph of Mitch in the chest pocket of his overalls. That's true, of course. McDelcott always had a photo of Mitch with him, but also one of my mom and me. It was in a small notebook with a transparent plastic insert where he kept all sorts of things, a ticket to a football game in Dallas, a few gas station receipts, a piece of a postcard with a stamp from Tanzania, and a curl of my mother's hair. She had told me about it on one of those evenings when she felt lonely enough to tell me some intimate things about herself and McDelcott. He had cut this off with a pocketknife when they were dating for the first time and made love in the Panhandle Motel on the road that leads to Dickens. He wished to have children one day, a real family, but it turned out that he was sterile, that something was wrong with his sperm, and so he carried photos of Mitch and me around as if he were our real father. He didn't mind showing the pictures around and saying these were his sons, but somebody who didn't know our family background or a stranger would have asked straight away how come he had these two different sons, one who looked Irish, and another who had dark skin. McDelcott almost certainly had to take a lot of abuse when he showed the photos because everybody knew well enough that Jim Fletcher was our father and not him. But he never let on, whatever the people said, and there was a lot of gossip in Winstel.

In any case, I don't believe Mitch is to blame for the fact that the truck skidded off the car jack and crushed McDelcott's rib cage as Ruby Rucker can be blamed for her husband cutting off half his foot while mowing the lawn. Who is to blame for an accident, anyway? After all, an accident is an accident simply because you're out of luck when it happens.

I tried to explain this to Mitch one time, but I don't think it sank in. In any case, Mitch tends to worry about a lot of things, so I'm not surprised he hasn't left me in peace ever since he found out I was writing a book.

Sometimes, when he was at home, he sneaked into my room, squatted down on the bed, and watched me write. Not that he wanted to read what I was writing. He can read, but he doesn't. You'd never see him reading a book. When mom is sitting in front of the TV, watching Elvis, he doesn't sit there with her, of course, because he doesn't feel like watching Elvis. But it would never occur to him to pick up a book. Instead, he sneaks around in the house, and into my room, and squats down on the bed behind me. He just sits there, listening to the clatter of my old typewriter, and when I lean back, letting my head fall back against the wall, because I've worn myself out, he would ask me in an entirely harmless way if I've written something about him and if I'll read it out to him. Of course, he knows that I'm writing about Lilly and about how I started my search for a man who we all presumed died in some prison.

After that autumn, when I returned to Winstel from Memphis, I could hardly wait for the summer, and the six weeks of vacation we would have then. That would be enough time to find a dead person, even if he was still alive.

In the meantime, I tried to get myself prepared. I tried to find out what happened to Crazy Legs, via the municipal authorities. They wrote back to me that no man named Bukka Harris was registered in Baton Rouge. "Sorry," they said. I wrote a letter to the prison administration in Fort Leavenworth and asked for documents relating to JB Swift. When I didn't get a written answer, I got on the phone. I was told that no JB or John B. Swift could be found in the computer system. Sorry again. I gave them more details. A few days later, I received a letter, telling me that JB Swift had been moved to San Quentin after a prison riot. I wrote to San Quentin. His name wasn't found there either. Not even when I gave them all the information I had and sent a copy of the transfer papers. It looked as if I wasn't getting anywhere. Consequently, I gave up writing or calling any of the authorities of the penal system. A few weeks later, in the middle of winter, the postman delivered a soiled envelope addressed to me. No return address. According to the postmark, it got sent from New Orleans, Louisiana. I took it to my room and opened it, making sure to do it when Mitch was gone. When I opened it, I found a small, yellowed newspaper clipping with a report that knocked me right out of my cowboy boots.

Under the headline "Free at Last," the report read as follows: "John B. Swift, a former legend of the blues, who shot a man on Beale Street, Memphis, in 1936, will be released today from the county prison in Hattiesburg. JB Swift has spent more than 40 years behind bars. In Fort Leavenworth, he was one of the ringleaders of a prison riot."

I called Hattiesburg straightaway. A woman there told me that a prisoner named Swift had died several years ago. I tried to dig deeper and asked when exactly he had died. She also said that they were unable to help me, as the old files had gotten destroyed in a fire in the archives.

I didn't give up and called again. I demanded to speak

to the prison warden.

A Mr. LeClair answered the phone. I asked him about JB, and to my surprise, he asked me whether I had something to do with the old lady, who, in the past, had called a few times from Memphis. I said no, and wanted to know from him what had happened to John B. Swift.

"What do you think happened? He died from pneumonia here in prison a few years ago."

"He was never released?"

"Released? No, I don't think so. But I've only been here for three years, and the old files and lists of inmates have all been — "

"Destroyed in a fire, I know," I snapped and slammed down the receiver. From that day on, I was pretty confident that JB was still alive. I started to long for the summer and vacation. I wanted to drive to Hattiesburg myself and find out what exactly had happened to JB and why they lied to me.

I didn't tell anybody about my research and the yellowed newspaper article, not even Lilly, who I talked to on the phone several times.

After school, all through the spring, I was either working at Jesse Walker's gas station or helping him in his car repair shop. I would need money to search for JB, for bus fares, lodging, and food. After all, Hattiesburg was a small city in the far south of Mississippi, not far from New Orleans, and not far from Baton Rouge either, the city on the Mississippi River where JB and Lilly had met for the first time. I looked at the map a hundred times as if I would be able to discover JB only by staring at the name of the small town long enough.

Mom went crazy when I told her about my plans. I had no choice but to tell her. Without her approval, I couldn't do anything. I would have had to slip off, but I didn't want to do that. And I couldn't, because of Mitch.

"Bradley, are you off your head?" she shouted. "JB's dead!"

"Then I'll find his grave."

"His grave! Now, listen carefully, son. I let you take that Greyhound to Memphis because I thought the old lady didn't need her dough anymore and would give you some of it. But since you've been back, you've been off your rocker. Do you think I haven't noticed? The old lady's memories went to your head. That's not okay. That's sick."

"What happened back then marked the beginning of my life, mom," I answered.

Her forehead wrinkled up, and she looked at me as if she was thinking about committing me to an asylum.

"The beginning of your life is the day your father created you in a fit of unbridled lust, Bradley. And if you want to know in detail how this could happen, I can only tell you that we were both pretty stupid at the time."

There was no point in arguing with my mother. I knew that she'd let me go anyway. And she knew it too. I had made my decision, and I wasn't going to let anybody stop me. Perhaps, secretly, she was hoping that I would change my mind. But then, we learned that Lilly would need an operation on her left eye in a few weeks, and mom thought it would be a good idea if I looked after her during the summer vacation, hoping again for the money the old lady must have stashed away. Apart from that, she only wanted to know if I had told my father about my decision to track down JB. I had tried it two or three times, but his phone was disconnected, and I didn't know where he was. I didn't care either. However, I did care. I missed him more than ever before, but I didn't want to admit it at the time.

So, on the second day of my vacation, I got on the Greyhound to Memphis, with all the money I had earned at Jesse Walker's in my pocket, and nothing else but my duffel bag. I had packed some gear, the book from Sara Carter's bookshop, the photos from the old days, and one picture of Lilly, which dad had taken on our first visit. I said goodbye to Hanna in the car park near the bus stop. She'd just won the county championship with her team and scored two goals in the final. Winstel celebrated her by hanging a banner across Main Street: "Hotspurs, way to go, Champs!" College team coaches got in touch with her. From Texas Christian, too, where she wanted to go because her father had studied there and belonged to a fraternity.

My mother came to the bus stop with me. As did Jesse Walker, in his dirty overalls, Wayne Bundy, and a few others I hung out with sometimes. I had only told them that I would go to Memphis to see my uncle and that I would probably stay there all summer. Hanna didn't want to understand. We hadn't spoken in five days because she was sulking. But when we said goodbye, she cried anyway.

"He's not going to war, Hanna," my mother tried to comfort her. "He'll be back in a few weeks." It was all in vain. The last thing I saw, when I was sitting on the bus looking back, was Hanna in the dust, waving the handkerchief full of tears, and Tex, Jesse Walker's dog, who was crazy about me, chasing the bus for almost three miles before he finally realized that his legs were too short or the bus was too fast.

I was on my way; my duffel bag stowed in the luggage net above my head. The seat next to me was empty. I made myself comfortable and read the book I had gotten in Sara Carter's bookstore; The Grapes of Wrath. When I started, I couldn't stop reading, and when I was too tired to read, I thought of Lilly. I could hardly wait to see her again.

CHAPTER 15
FIFTY YEARS

I had written to let her know I would be visiting.

"Since she's known you were coming, she's very erratic," said Rhonda, who accompanied me upstairs to put some drops in Lilly's left eyes, which was operated on three weeks previously. "The surgery turned out well, but she's very impatient because she still can't see well."

When we entered the room, she was sitting by the window. She had a weird little plastic cup over her left eye, attached to her face with adhesive tape.

"Lilly, look who's here," said Rhonda.

Lilly turned her head and looked at me with her healthy eye.

"It's me, Bradley," I said.

She grumbled. Rhonda threw a meaningful glance at me.

"I'll put the drops in your eye now, Lilly," she said.

"Drops? What on earth for?" Lilly shouted. "None of this helps anyway. They'll have to operate again. I've already told the doctor."

"The operation went perfectly, Lilly. In a few weeks, the eye will be all right."

"I don't have that much time! A few weeks... Who knows, anything can happen in a few weeks."

"Please hold your head back, Lilly so that I can put the drops in your eye."

"Stupid drops," Lilly grumbled. "I hardly recognize you. The eye they operated on doesn't see a thing, and the other one is almost blind."

She leaned her head back, and Rhonda put a precise number of drops through the hole in the plastic cup directly into Lilly's eye.

"Well, I'll leave you two alone," Rhonda said.

When she had left the room, I asked Lilly if she wanted to come to the garden with me.

"The way I'm dressed?"

"You're dressed perfectly fine."

"The way I'm dressed, I'm not going anywhere."

"All right, then we'll stay here," I said and sat down on the edge of the bed.

"Thanks for the letters," she said after a while. "This Sara Carter, she must be a witch, Bradley. Watch out for her. I know people like that. There were a lot of them in the old days, in particular among the blacks. They never leave you alone, not even when you're dead."

I had no idea what had happened to her since I had last seen her. She appeared distracted and impatient, and I didn't succeed in getting close to her. I tried to turn the conversation to JB, but she refused to pick up on it. I stayed on it, though. I asked if she had ever heard anything from JB's friends. She clammed up even more and turned away from me.

Finally, I gave up. Downstairs, I asked Rhonda what was the matter with her.

"She's not doing as well as she did last year, Bradley. That's the case with many people here. Sometimes, they become depressed. They feel abandoned and become lonely. Lilly has never been one who laughs easily.

And she hasn't made many friends here among us. And none of the few friends she did make are around anymore. Sophie is the only one left. She looks after your grandmother, but she's over seventy herself and has problems of her own."

"Has Lilly s son Lewis been here lately?"

"No. Sometimes he calls and talks to her, but I don't think he truly connects with your grandmother."

"But he's her son, isn't he?"

Rhonda smiled but didn't say anything.

At dinner, I asked Uncle Lewis why he never visited Lilly. I didn't want it to sound like blame, but it probably sounded like it to him anyway.

"Bradley, your grandmother much rather would see your father than me," he said. "That's always been the case."

"Because she never liked you," said Lizette spitefully. "Because she didn't like you, or your father."

Uncle Lewis's face turned hard. He didn't say a word.

I kept silent and lowered my head, poking around my plate and wishing I could disappear.

"She conceived you from a man she didn't love. I can understand why she's never liked you, I mean. I can understand that well enough."

"That's enough, Liz," Uncle Lewis said. I noticed that his voice was trembling.

"It's true, Lewis," said his wife. "You're the only one who doesn't want to accept it. She loves your half-brother, this good-for-nothing tramp, who left his family because of some broad — "

"That's enough now!" Uncle Lewis slammed his fist on the table so hard that the plates jumped. "Bradley doesn't need to worry about these things when he's here, Liz."

"Why shouldn't he know the truth? We have to live with it. It's been like this for so long." She turned directly toward me. "Your uncle is almost fifty years old and cannot get over the fact that he was an unwanted child."

Uncle Lewis got up from his chair and walked out into the garden. I had also lost my appetite. I excused myself and went upstairs to my room.

Later, somebody knocked on the door. It was Aunt Liz. Her eyes were red. "I'm sorry, Bradley, but sometimes I just can't bear it," she said. "I'm sorry."

"It's all right," I told her.

She noticed that I was in the middle of packing my things.

"Where are you going?"

"Away," I said.

She called for Uncle Lewis. After a while, he came into the house. He looked as if he'd had all he could take.

"Bradley wants to leave," Liz told him.

"Where to?" he asked.

"Away," I said.

He looked at me and understood that I couldn't stay there.

"Should I call your mother?" he asked.

"No."

"Anyone else?"

"No, nobody."

"But somebody needs to know where you are and what's going on."

I assured him that I'd call my mother myself. I spent the night at their house, but the next morning, when they had both gone, I left. I was kind of mixed up and took the bus to the retirement home to talk to Grandmother one more time. She was in better shape than the day before, and I knew straight away I could rely on her strength to carry out my plan.

"I'm driving to Hattiesburg today," I said casually.

She looked up.

"Why are you going there? They told you he's dead, too, didn't they?"

"Why do you say too, Grandma?"

"Me?" She turned her head to the side.

"You've called there a few times, haven't you?"

She didn't answer. I told her what I was told over the phone; that a lady from Memphis had called several times and had asked about JB.

Lilly lifted her head, looked at me, and attempted to smile.

"What do you want to be when you're grown up, Bradley? A detective?"

"An author," I said and pulled the small newspaper clipping from my trouser pocket. I had kept it in a clear sleeve for credit cards. "What were you told when you called?"

"The same thing they told you."

"That he died in prison?"

"Yes, that he's dead."

"Here, Grandma. This article was published in a newspaper more than ten years ago."

I held it toward her so that she could look at it with her healthy eye. She was able to decipher the headline.

"Free at Last," she said quietly and listened as if she was waiting for an echo. But it stayed quiet in her little room, and she grabbed the newspaper clipping with a trembling hand. "They — set him free," she said so quietly that I could barely make out her words. "Please, Bradley, read out to me what it says."

I knew the lines by heart and didn't even need to read them.

"John B. Swift, a former legend of the blues, who, in 1936, shot a man on Beale Street, Memphis, will be released today from the county prison in Hattiesburg. JB Swift has spent more than forty years behind bars. He was one of the ringleaders of a prison riot in Fort Leavenworth."

Lilly stared at the newspaper clipping.

"Why would they have lied to us there in Hattiesburg, Bradley?" she asked after a few seconds.

"I don't know. I don't even know who sent me this newspaper clipping. It arrived in an envelope without a return address. There was no note. It was from New Orleans."

"Do you know anybody there?"

"No."

"And your father?"

"What about him?"

"Would it be possible that he sent you this newspaper

article?"

"Why should he have done that? He doesn't even know that I've decided to look for JB. I haven't heard from him in over a year."

"Well, then I don't know who could have sent you this clipping, Bradley. Would you do a favor for me and read it out to me again?"

I told her again, word for word, what was written in the short article. And she tried yet again to look for the meaning.

"If he was released ten years ago, he couldn't have died in prison," she finally said.

"Right, Grandma. This article is either a newspaper hoax, and JB was never released, or he's still alive."

"If — if JB is still alive, why has he never…" She stopped talking, because she could have answered her question herself. In all those years, JB had never called, not once. But not because he had forgotten her; he hadn't called because he was ashamed of all he had done to her. That's the way he was. Lilly had told me that JB couldn't bear having destroyed her life. That's why she didn't tell him she was pregnant with his child, knowing it would have made his life in prison even worse. Fifty years went by, years full of yearning and hopes. Years of secret love, and a fire that never went out.

I promised Lilly that afternoon, and for the second time, I would find him. I also promised myself. I wanted to know where I had come from on the long way to the present. Where everything began and where, perhaps, I could find my father again on the day he was born.

CHAPTER 16
FORREST COUNTY JAIL

Before we moved to Winstel, we had lived in Tennessee, near Memphis to be precise, and I remember an Elvis song my mother always turned up when it was playing on the radio. It told the story of a kid (I assumed it was Elvis himself) who asked a phone operator for a girl's address. He only knew the girl's name and that she lived on the other side of the Mississippi.

The song begins like this: "Long distance information, give me Memphis, Tennessee…"

I couldn't recall how the lyrics continued, though I had listened to it so many times. Maybe because, later on, we moved to Texas, and mom never played the record again.

It was our dad who wanted to go to Texas. One day, he came home angry. He rarely got into that kind of state, and when I was lying in bed, unable to fall asleep, I heard him say to Mother: "Then we'll just leave," to which she responded: "But where should we go?" He didn't have an answer for a while, but finally, he said: "Texas!" And then, or so it sounded, he had made up his mind to move to Texas with mother and me and start all over. Only later did I find out the real reason he was so upset that day. He and Lewis had fought because of Grandma, who, several days before, had suffered something like a small stroke and had been lying in a municipal hospital, unable to talk properly because some facial muscles got temporarily paralyzed. They fought because Lewis and Lizette insisted on placing Lilly in a retirement facility, while my father reminded them that they were living in a house that belonged to my grandmother. He suggested to them that they should thankful and pick up my grandmother, and care for her. But Aunt Lizette, who never had a child of her own and sometimes suffered from depression, wouldn't have any of it. So it came to a fight because there was no room in our house. Father didn't have a job at the time, and only my mom earned a bit of money, mainly with sewing work.

Texas. That's where we wanted to go. There, everything was supposed to take a turn for the better. No Uncle Lewis nearby. No Liz, who was beside herself most of the time anyway. And no Grandma either, for whom my father, or so he probably believed, wouldn't feel responsible anymore once he put a few hundred miles between them.

And so we packed our stuff, all our gear, some of which is still lying around our house today and took the Greyhound to Texas. I don't remember much about the trip. Only a few images remain in my head. Fragments of a journey into the night, the vague visual memento of a man sitting on the other side of the aisle of the bus, snoring. Of lights, flickering by outside. Of a traffic policeman, who stopped the bus and talked to the driver through the window. Of the moon, hanging in the sky like a sickle. And of my mother's eyes, betraying her hope to hide that she was scared.

When she thought I was asleep, she whispered to my father, and I opened one of my eyes a little and blinked over at them. He had put one arm around my mother, and her head was leaning against his shoulder, and she was crying.

"Everything will be all right," I heard him say, and this was the last time I saw them like that. All he was telling her was a lie because nothing turned out right. He left barely half a year later. I don't know if he was aware that she was pregnant. He just walked out.

On the trip to Hattiesburg, on Interstate 55, a lot of things went through my head. Mitch's birth, which took place at our house in Texas. I often thought I should have done something to prevent our father from leaving. Today, of course, I know its all nonsense. I'm well aware that certain things in life can't be changed. And that one has to have some bad luck to recognize when happiness finally comes along.

I arrived at Hattiesburg in the middle of the night, just before eleven. Some cops were taking a close look at the people getting off the bus. They noticed right away that a kid got off the Greyhound who couldn't be of age and wasn't being picked up by anybody. They stopped me outside in the parking lot, where two patrol cars were parked.

"I assume you want to visit relatives here, son," one of them said.

"Correct," I said.

"Who exactly, if I may ask?"

"My grandfather."

"And what's your grandfather's name?"

"John B. Swift."

One of them didn't have a clue who that was, but the

other thought he had heard the name before.

"And where is your grandfather supposed to live?"

"In the can," I said.

"In prison?"

"Yes, in the county jail."

They grinned. "Which one? There are three — one in Lamar County, one in Forrest County, and one in Perry County, which is a few miles farther east."

"In Forrest County jail," I said.

"That's where you want to go?"

"Yes, sir."

They looked at my duffel bag.

"On foot?"

"First of all, I'm going there," I said, pointing to a neon sign on the other side of the street, hanging above the entrance to a motel.

"Do you have any money?"

"Yes, sir. I'm not homeless. I didn't run away from home, either. If you want to, you can call my mother, in Winstel, Texas. The number is — "

"We'd rather you told us what your grandfather did," one of them interrupted me.

"He shot a man more than fifty years ago."

"Your grandfather is a killer?"

"He killed a man who had clubbed him with a baseball bat. As the man was white and my grandfather black, they put my grandfather behind bars and threw away the key."

They both were black, and they stared at me.

"Your grandfather isn't white?"

"No," I grinned. "He's black."

"You don't look it, son. You look pretty pale."

"That's how I always turn when cops grill me in the middle of the night."

They laughed. One of them walked to the police car and made a phone call. When he came back, I could tell he knew something.

"Kid, I have bad news for you."

"He's dead, right? They told you that John B. Swift had died?"

He shook his head.

"No, that's not what I was told. They told me that your grandfather doesn't want to see anybody."

My ears heard something my brain didn't seem able to register. I was stunned and felt my knees wanting to collapse.

"Then he's still alive," I heard myself say.

"You didn't know that?" The two cops seemed a bit confused. "Why did you come here, if you thought he was dead?"

"I... I was certain he was still alive."

They shook their heads as if I had been talking to them in a foreign language.

"You came here because you were certain he was still alive, but now you're surprised that he is alive? Tell me, son, do you think you still have all your marbles?"

"My mother asks me that question all the time," I said. Slowly, I managed to get a grip. I asked them whether I was allowed to leave now, and they said it would be okay, but that I should return to Memphis the next morning on the first Greyhound because my grandfather wouldn't want to see me anyway. I thanked them for the well-meant advice, shouldered my duffel bag and, under the cops' watchful eyes, marched across the street to the Talahalla Motel. It was a run-down dive, but then again, the room only cost seventeen bucks. It smelled terrible, and somebody made a racket next door all night as if two monsters were busy devouring each other. I didn't sleep well. I dreamt of cops throwing me into the sea from a big boat. And of a cave filled with human skeletons, and of a naked woman who turned to stone when I touched her.

The next morning, I woke early, tried to fall asleep again, but there were noises in my head, and I failed when I tried to think of nothing. So I tried to think of Alesha, but I couldn't find any rest. After a while, I just got up and left the motel, without washing myself or brushing my teeth. I got a taxi to Forrest County Jail and entered visitor's reception room through the glass door. At the desk, I asked for John.

"John?" asked a uniformed, dark-skinned civil servant who looked at me suspiciously. "I'd assume that there are a whole bunch of people here whose first names are John."

"John B. Swift," I said. "Tell him that I'm here. My name is Bradley Fletcher."

"I thought it must be you," she sighed, shaking her head. "You didn't believe me when I told you he's dead, right?"

"Was that you on the phone?"

"Yes."

"Did you lie to me?"

"Yes."

"Why?"

"Because he's asked me to."

I remained silent because I didn't know what to say. She could probably tell that I was pretty confused. An almost motherly expression came into her eyes.

"You need to understand, Bradley," she said. "The old man doesn't want to be reminded of what happened a long time ago. He's finished with that life and…"

"Finished?" I gasped. "The old man doesn't even know he has a son and that I'm his grandson. And he wants to be finished with his life?" I was on the verge of tears. "I want to see him!" I struggled to get the words out. "Where is he? Didn't they release him from prison a long time ago?"

She took a deep breath. She probably realized that she couldn't hold me back.

"Please, sit down over there," she said. "It'll take a few minutes."

I didn't sit down. I couldn't. I set my duffel bag on the bench and started pacing up and down the room. She talked to somebody on the phone. When she had finished, she began to flick through some files. But every time I glanced over at her, I noticed her observing me. As if I was locked up in here; as if she were afraid of the danger lurking inside me; a tiger in a cage. And I must admit that I felt an incredible anger welling up inside me and would have loved to kick my feet against the walls.

Minutes passed, testing my patience, but finally, a door opened at the rear of the visitor's reception room, where the Star - Spangled Banner and the Mississippi state flag flanked the picture of our president. And when I caught sight of the man, this gaunt, gray-haired man in blue overalls, I knew that I hadn't covered all those miles in vain. I had reached the end of my journey and had no other desire than to have had Lilly there with me.

The old man, who was standing in the door, as if he didn't dare take the next step, was my grandfather.

JB.

I wanted to walk toward him, but my feet wouldn't obey my commands. There I stood, unable to move.

His gaze was firmly fixed on me, but I wasn't sure if he saw me. He hesitated when he stepped into the room and carefully shut the door behind him. Then he came toward me, walking upright and with supple grace, in a manner I had never seen before in an old man. Only the gray hair, which was cut short, and the marks of life I could see on his face, reminded me that JB must have been around eighty.

"You never give up, do you?" he said.

I nodded. I wanted to reply to his question with one tiny but powerful word, but I couldn't form a sound for quite a while.

"Never," I finally said.

He smiled. "I can tell from your eyes," he said. "Lilly's eyes."

I had to laugh, couldn't stop for a half of a minute or so, and he studied me patiently till I found my composure again.

"What did I say?" he wanted to know.

"You're wrong," I said. "Lilly says they're yours."

CHAPTER 17
ON BROKEN WINGS

If I thought I had reached the end of my journey there at Forrest County Jail, I was soon proven wrong. JB was standing in front of me, in the flesh, alive and visibly doing well. But suddenly, I wasn't so sure anymore why I had visited in the first place. You see, he didn't want to leave. He told me so right away as we arrived in a small waiting room with two maroon armchairs, a small table with a coffee machine, a water fountain, and an ashtray. There were no windows, and the air conditioner blew freezing air straight at my neck.

"I wouldn't take a bet on me leaving this place if I'd be you, for this prison is my home," JB said after closing the door and walking toward the coffee machine.

I was standing in the middle of the room. Of course, I hadn't been prepared to hear that someone could feel at home in a prison.

"Do you want a coffee?" he asked.

"No."

"Then sit down."

I sat on one of the chairs and watched him pour coffee into a Styrofoam cup, add sugar, some milk, and then stir with a little plastic spoon. He did everything as if he had done it a thousand times before. Every movement seemed to come out perfect, and everything looked neat and straightforward somehow.

When he had finished, he turned to me, the cup in his left hand. I noticed that immediately, left-handed myself—in fact, the only one in my family except for JB.

Minutes passed. Neither one of us said anything. I waited for JB to give me some speech about life, but he remained silent, sipping his coffee while he looked at me briefly several times, not the way you look at someone you want to take the measure of, but the way you look at someone you don't want to have much to do with.

His look annoyed me.

"Somebody told Lilly you were dead," I said.

He lifted his head. Now he was looking straight at me. "As you can see, I'm alive."

I nodded. "Why the hell would you joke about it?"

"About what?" he asked, wrinkling his forehead.

"About life and death," I answered.

He took a sip of coffee and seemed thoroughly pleased. "Did Lilly send you?"

"No."

"Your father?"

"He doesn't even know I'm here, and I don't know where he is. Do you know who I am?"

"Of course, I know who you are." He chuckled as if amused by his thoughts.

"Wrong."

He looked at me with curiosity in his eyes. "Wrong? And who are you if you aren't Lilly's grandchild?"

I had him where I wanted him. "Yours," I said, thinking something might happen to him, that he would go weak for a second or something, but either he was hard-hearted, or he didn't understand what I was saying.

"I'm also your grandchild, Mr. JB Swift."

"That's true," he said, without batting an eye.

It almost knocked me over. I stared at him, stunned. I assumed that he had no clue Lilly was pregnant when he got busted.

"You know who I am?"

He didn't answer. He only gave a cryptic smile, and his face's spotted, wrinkly skin looked like an impenetrable mask, made from the root of an old oak tree that had been struck by lightning and felled by the wind.

I'd need a giant bulldozer to make him leave this place.

"Who told you who I am?"

"Friends."

"Joey Pickett? The one-eyed man?"

"Joey Pickett? What do you know about Joey?"

"Lilly told me about him. And about all the others. Apart from that, I've been to Sara Carter's bookshop on South Lauderdale."

He squinted. Memories seemed to be stirring inside him. I didn't take my eyes off him. He put the cup on the table and hooked his thumbs into the flap of his overalls. He smiled because it gave him something to hide behind.

"If Lilly didn't send you, then why did you come here?"

This question came a little too early. "Lilly told me everything that happened," I said evasively.

"What's everything?"

"Everything. From the beginning."

He took a breath. I imagined him thinking about how everything began. About the restaurant in Baton Rouge, where they had seen each other for the first time. And how he had boldly walked from the bar into the dining room and right up to the table she was sitting at with her parents, and how he handed her the rose.

"Lilly still has the rose," I said. "The petals, that is."

His eyes hardened and returned to me. "She should have thrown them away."

"Not Lilly. For her, that would have been a sin."

He bowed his head. I left him to his thoughts and remained quiet. It took a long time before he looked up and lifted the cup. He took a sip and put the cup down again, but he made no move to resume the conversation.

"Why do they say you died, when you are still alive?"

"I asked the people here to say I had."

"Why?"

"Because…" His skin seemed to get too tight for him. Even though the room was cold, sweat glistened in the wrinkles on his forehead.

"Lilly is living in a retirement home in Memphis," I said. "Not far from Beale Street. The home is called Harvest Moon. Once in a while, I visit her, and she tells me about the past. She thought you were dead, but she didn't want to believe it. Her uncertainty has kept you alive, I guess."

He did not answer, just looked at me.

"Somebody sent me a newspaper clipping about your release from this prison. That happened several years ago, almost ten, I believe. Why are you still here?"

"Where should I go?"

"Out!"

He laughed out loud. "I've been out."

"And why are you inside again?"

"Because I didn't like it outside."

"I don't believe you. Whatever there is in here, it has to be better outside."

"For you, sure. Outside, that is your world. You're familiar with it. When you cross the street, you arrive safely on the other side. When I walked out of this prison and crossed the street, there was chaos, and some people in the cars wanted to kill me because I did everything wrong."

I had to laugh. "What did you do wrong?"

"If I only knew. But nobody told me. They shouted at me and shook their fists, but nobody told me what I'd done wrong, so I still don't know and would do everything wrong again if I ever left."

"Not if you walk out of here with me."

He shook his head. "You wouldn't want me to do that, Bradley."

"Why not?"

"Because there is no point," he said. "I stay here. You can also tell Lilly. Please tell her that I'm doing well and that I'm waiting for the day we'll see each other again. That's not so far away now, I believe."

They were both alive, but waiting for death as if it would make the day of dying the most rewarding day of their lives. I refused to understand. For me, life was the most valuable thing, with time playing no part. I was alive. Now.

"Lilly won't be dying for a long time," I consequently

said. "It's true that she had a small stroke a few years ago, but now she's her old self again. She's even had her eye operated on."

"Which one?"

"The left one."

The wrinkles on his face seemed to smooth while he thought of Lilly's face, the face he knew so well.

"She doesn't believe I can get you to come with me to Memphis," I said.

"She knows me well. Nobody knows me better."

"She knows you the way you were," I contradicted. "If she saw you this despondent, it would be a great disappointment considering the courage we both thought you had."

He raised his eyebrows and if nothing else he did seem to realize I had spent time thinking about him, about Lilly and the life they hadn't been allowed to live together. I believe he sensed that he wouldn't get rid of me so quickly because I was of his blood.

"You think I don't have any courage?"

"I don't think that. But you are afraid of the outside world."

"Are you suggesting I shouldn't be?" he asked mockingly. "You can't break a bird's wings, then put him on a branch and expect him to fly."

"I can imagine that it isn't easy to return to freedom after fifty years in the can. But I'm asking myself what's worse, to be squashed by the world outside or to kick the bucket in here."

He was not ready to answer right away. I waited.

"Aren't you afraid of the future, Bradley?" he finally asked just as the next question was forming on my tongue. He'd turned the tables.

Of course, I'd been worried about the future — a young person is entitled to look into the future with concern. On the other hand, when I had been on the water tower with Wayne, and it was getting dark, I sometimes imagined my future shining as brightly as the stars above the Rimrocks. But during the day, when I saw how my mother and other people lived in Winstel, I was sometimes scared of what Mr. Ledbetter called a decent life.

JB seemed to be guessing my thoughts.

"I wasn't afraid of the future when I was a young man. The first time I felt fear I bought a pistol. I was the happiest man back then, but it all stopped with a pistol shot. Here, inside the prison, I've given up thinking about the future, because there was none. It's lurking outside and doesn't like me. I found that out quickly."

"You happened to be all alone when they released you from prison. Now, I'm here! Forget the future. It's here and now. I have a whole load of it left to deal with in the future. But you, you're an old man now, too old to be choosy, trust me!"

He had to laugh, and I laughed with him. That might have been our bridge to each other. And I had Lilly with me. My Grandma Lilly, in a way he didn't know her. I took out the photograph my father had taken of her. A Polaroid. I looked at it briefly, then got up and put it on the table near the coffee machine.

JB took a look at it and lifted his head again right away.

"What do you want from me, Bradley?"

"I want to talk to you. I want to hear your story of a young, fearless bluesman called The Legend and what happened to him since. I want to know everything."

"Why?"

"Because I'm your blood."

He took a deep breath, took the photograph from the table and looked at it again. His hand was trembling a little, and he didn't seem to need glasses to look at Lilly's face. I watched him but was unable to make out any emotion. While I observed him, there was still my voice inside my head, like a trapped echo. *Because I'm your blood.* No idea why I had said it. *Your blood.* Nobody would say something like that anymore, not in a moment like that. It sounded pompous, but the words just came to me, and I spoke them before I could change my mind.

He put the photograph on the table.

"You knew all along, didn't you? You knew that Lilly was pregnant when they sent you to Fort Leavenworth?"

"I suspected it," JB said. "I didn't know. But when I saw her for the last time, there was something in her eyes I had never seen before. Not only the pain and the sadness, but also the certainty to have found a new strength."

"But she didn't tell you."

"No. We never talked again."

"Why?"

He seemed to turn the question over in his head.

He probably had asked himself often over the past fifty years, but now he was thinking about how to make me understand.

"I believe we didn't want to destroy our love, Bradley," he said. "And I also think that we've succeeded. At least, I've succeeded; I know that much. If Lilly hadn't been with me every day, every minute of my life, every step of the way, I probably wouldn't have survived. I don't know if you can understand that, Bradley. It certainly can't be easy for you, coming here from the outside, and able to leave again. With all the strength she found in her despair, she had given me hope when they put me behind bars, and the strength to survive."

"And all this is what I don't understand, considering you could just go see her."

"I see her, Bradley, the way she's stayed in my memory."

"That's not real," I objected.

"For a prisoner, memories are the only reality worth living for."

"Aren't there any bad memories?"

"Yes, they are a part of it. And sometimes my memories turn into nightmares."

I didn't need to ask him what his worst nightmare was. I think it started at the moment when he pulled the revolver from his jacket and pointed it at the man.

"Lilly also lives through her memories," I said.

"Lilly." He raised his eyebrow. "Let's talk about her, Bradley. How is she?"

"She's fine."

"Tell me about her."

"In here?" I looked around. "I can't breathe in here."

His eyes became alert once more. He opened his mouth to say something, but then didn't say a word.

"How is it that we can talk to each other without being watched?" I asked.

"I've already told you that I'm not a prisoner in here anymore."

"Not a prisoner? What's that supposed to mean? Is this a prison or an old folks' home?"

His face didn't give anything away. "I'm in here of my own free will."

"They released you, and you returned voluntarily? You got to explain that to me."

He didn't dodge my derisive look. On the contrary, his eyes hardened.

"I'm the janitor here."

"The janitor?"

"That's my job. I get paid for doing it. I can live in here. And when I want to leave, I can do so anytime."

JB took the photo from the table, walked past me to the door, and grasped the doorknob with his left hand.

"I'm left-handed too," I said quickly.

He grinned. "You are my blood," he said, reminding me of my own words. Then he opened the door.

"I must go back to work. The people here don't pay me for doing nothing."

"You said you could leave anytime. Why don't we go to McDonald's for a Big Mac? I do that with Lilly sometimes. We go to McDonald's near the retirement home, and the walls there are full of old photos of the great blues musicians that used to play on Beale Street. When we're there, we talk about you most of the time."

He let the Polaroid of Lilly disappear in the breast pocket of his overalls and opened the door wider. I got up and walked out into the visitor's reception room. The clerk at the desk followed me with her eyes. I grinned at her.

"We can talk about Lilly at McDonald's," I said to JB.

"You never give up, do you?"

"Never," I said.

He scratched his neck, wrinkled his brow, and gave me a wry look. "Okay," he said. "Wait here a moment."

I could have shouted for joy, but I tried to stay calm. He walked out the same door he'd come through earlier, while I walked up to the reception desk and leaned on the marble top.

"A great jail you have here," I said through the glass, which prevented me from planting a kiss on the officer's cheek out of sheer joy. "Where I come from, we don't have one."

"Where is it you come from?"

"Winstel."

"Winstel. Never heard of it."

"It's a sleepy town in Texas where nothing ever happens. In the old days, there was a prison, but that is a long time ago."

She looked at me strangely, unable to figure out what I meant, but I didn't explain myself. I sat down on the bench and waited, thinking back to the day I'd helped Santiago Gomez break out of prison.

CHAPTER 18
YESTERDAY MAN

Deputy Paul Rinetti had caught him down in the Brewster Valley. A yearling had been killed on the grazing land of the Brewster Ranch two days earlier. The little steer had gotten lost among the headwaters of the South Wichita River, roughly thirty miles from Winstel. Brewster's cowboys had seen the vultures and then found parts of the dead animal. Somebody must have killed it with a knife, with one slice through the carotid artery. The steer had been carefully carved up, apparently by someone who'd done it before. Most of the meat was gone. What remained lay scattered all around the spot where the animal got slaughtered.

Fresh tracks led into the briar thicket near the old oil field, where a few derricks were still standing, though they hadn't pumped oil for a long time. There, the cowboys bumped into a group of Mexican border jumpers who surrendered when they got surrounded. Only one ran off. A boy, hardly older than Mitch. He ran as fast as he could, straight into the thicket, and the cowboys shot a few bullets at him. Then they tried chasing him, but the thicket was nearly impassable for the horses. The boy escaped, and the Cowboys drove the others to the road, loaded them onto a pickup and took them to Dickens, where the border patrol was based.

Deputy Rinetti, who was serving in Winstel in those days and hardly ever had anything to do, didn't want to miss the chance to be a hero. He drove his pickup to the briar thicket and found the boy, as he was washing the blood off his body in a pond of the Brewster Valley, not far from Winstel. He took him back to town, and even though everyone asked him to give the boy something to eat and then let him go, Rinetti locked him up in a cell.

That night, Wayne and I visited Jesse Walker. He had a set of picklocks we stole out of his shop when he wasn't paying attention. One of them fit the cell's lock. We got the boy out, led him to Jesse Walker's shop, and hid him in one of the small shed behind the house. Rinetti was looking for him everywhere and cursed and threatened not to rest until he'd punished those responsible for the prisoner's escape.

But he never found out. The boy, Santiago Gomez, stayed in Jesse Walker's shed for seven days, without anyone noticing. Not even Jesse knew, although he often went outside and peed against the wall of the small shed, where the old, bald tires were rotting in the sun.

We became friends, Santiago, Wayne and I, but one morning, when we came to the shed, he had gone. We felt abandoned that day. Pretty empty. In the evening, we climbed up the metal ladder to the water tank and looked out into the countryside, knowing full well that we wouldn't see him. But he had to be somewhere out there, and I wished I could be out there with him, far from Winstel, in a place where there were no streets, no houses. The loneliness out there tempted me more than it scared me, and only when the sun had set, and dusk rested into my soul did fear creep up inside me — fear of being alone, fear of never seeing my mother again, never entering our house again, never talking to my father on the phone again.

"Come on, let's go," Wayne finally said. He hadn't said a word while we sat up there because he'd been lost in his thoughts and was probably taking as deep a look into himself as I had.

We climbed down the ladder and went home. Three days later, we heard that a farmer had been killed on the open road, near Dumont, in the northeastern corner of the county. Presumably, with his revolver. When a couple of grouse hunters found him, he lived just long enough to say that a young Mexican had attacked him. The killer, Wayne and I guessed, must be our friend Santiago Gomez.

The entire county went into a panic. Barely two days later border patrol officers caught him at a narrow gorge called Rimrock-Gap near the Twin Buttes. He had built a fire at night to keep warm, but it gave him away. In the cold gray of dawn, they cornered him. When he ran, they shot him down.

I told JB the story on the way to McDonald's after I'd recovered from seeing the way he looked in his street clothes. He would have fit better in a Hollywood movie set in Al Capone's time than in present-day Hattiesburg.

Brown pinstripe trousers, white shirt, tie suspenders, and a hat. JB draped the jacket that matched the trousers over his arm.

It was brutally humid, so close to the Gulf of Mexico. Nobody else was wearing a tie and suspenders. The people we encountered were wearing jeans, T-shirts, and sneakers. Little, sweaty children looked at JB with curious eyes. Women, smelling of deodorant, stared at the old man while walking past. A few boys and girls in front of McDonald's saw us coming and scrutinized us, passing around a bag of French fries and sipping Coke from large cups.

"Hey, what's with that old guy?" one of them asked.

"With what old guy?" I asked.

"With that one over there." He pointed his cup at JB. "He looks pretty much like a leftover piece of crap from yesteryear."

I grinned stupidly enough for them to take me for one of their kind. "He's the Yesterday Man," I said coolly and left them behind. I knew JB had heard what the kid had said, but he didn't seem to care.

While at McDonald's, JB didn't say a single word. I could sense his vigilance as if he were expecting a trap. An alarm was probably sounding inside him all the time. He seemed to wait for something to happen, but nothing did. Nobody honked at us when we crossed the street on a green light barely making it before it turned red again. The kids in front of McDonald's had shown no inclination of getting rough. The girl we ordered our Big Macs from had put on a radiant smile and asked JB whether he wanted extra ketchup. A little girl walked past our table, bent down and picked up JB's jacket, which had fallen from the seat without him noticing. Nobody entered while shooting a gun either, as had happened recently in San Diego or some other such place — something I had imagined ever since I'd read about it in the paper.

Of course, I felt triumphant while sitting at the table eating french-fries and our burgers, drinking our icy cold Cokes. It was an altogether happy experience. The world was showing itself in its best light to JB as if it had been waiting for a reunion with one of its many lost sons of times past.

A lovely, perfect world it seemed to be. Everything was cool.

"So what do you think?" I asked him. "This is my world."

He lifted his head, with ketchup in the corner of his mouth. I could see his white stubble glistening in the light, even though he had just shaved.

"Not bad, is it?" I teased him. He took a short glance at me. Looked like he wanted to make sure I didn't feel responsible for creating the world. Then he swayed his head, looking at the rest of his burger, which had become soggy, almost dissolving between his ketchup-covered fingers.

"This is a Big Mac?" he asked.

"Yes. Lilly loves Big Macs."

"Why?" He gave me a serious look. "Doesn't she have any teeth left?"

The way he had said this rubbed me the wrong way. I wanted to set him straight and explain to him that Lilly was an incredible woman when his face broke into a thousand wrinkles.

"Lilly without teeth," he said and burst out laughing. "You know how often we imagined how it would be to grow old together. It would have never occurred to me that Lilly would lose her teeth."

"But she hasn't!" I grumbled. "And Lilly is…"

"A beautiful woman," he interrupted me, laughing. "Don't get all worked up, kid. I just can't imagine Lilly enjoying this kind of food. She loved to accompany me to my place so we could cook together."

"She'd eat her burger before it goes bad."

The rest of the burger slipped through his fingers and fell back onto the tray. He grabbed a napkin. "I know what Lilly looks like," he said. "Perhaps you think I've only known since I saw the photograph, but the photograph is only a picture. For me, Lilly hasn't remained the way she was then. Even at the risk of you not getting this or thinking I'm crazy, I'm telling you that Lilly has aged with me, and I don't even need to close my eyes to see her. That's why I laughed. Lilly without teeth, that's funny."

He was a little like my father.

I realized he was having trouble cleaning his fingers. "The restroom's over there," I said. "McDonald's is renowned for its clean restrooms."

When he came out of the toilette, the kids came inside. One of the girls asked him whether he had anything to do with the movies. They wanted to know if he was a Hollywood movie star. JB shook his head.

"Once upon a time, I was a blues musician," he said.

Confused, the girl looked at her friends. One of the boys turned toward JB.

"Blues, man, that's gone. Us niggers dig rap now, and

that's all there is."

"That's obvious," JB replied with a smile and came to the table, where I had opened the book from Sara Carter's bookshop. He sat down, saw the book, and took his glasses out of his jacket, put them on, and looked at the photo.

"Where did you get that from?"

"From Sara Carter's bookshop."

He studied the photo briefly, and then raised his head. "I never knew what had happened with my things," he said. He didn't say a word about the man in the picture. He didn't mention the guitar hanging behind him on the wall either, even though he'd noticed it. He closed the book and handed it to me. "Come on. Let's go."

We left McDonald's. Outside, I asked him where he wanted to go, and he said he'd go anywhere with me but Memphis.

"It's your world, Bradley. You lead me through it, and I'll take a look, and while we're at it, you tell me about Lilly."

"And then?"

"Then what?"

"When I've told you everything?"

"Then we'll go home."

"And me? What about me? If you believe I'll drive back to Memphis without you, you've got another thing coming. And I also won't go back to Winstel. I'm staying here until you're not afraid anymore of going back to Memphis and meet Lilly."

He said nothing after that. We went down Main Street

in the sticky heat of the day, and I told him about Lilly. I also told him about mom and dad and Mitch and Mr. McDelcott and the people of Winstel. Now and then, he interrupted me and asked me questions — whether I had a girl, for example. I said her name was Hanna and that she played soccer. He was surprised by that. He wanted to know a lot about my father, but there wasn't much I wanted to tell him. I withheld the truth about what happened with Alesha. He didn't need to know. I didn't tell him that my father had left us at a difficult time, my mom being pregnant, without even saying goodbye. I only told him that something had gone wrong between him and mom and that they split up, and that, later on, my mom married another man. I told him about the Rimrocks, and how the cliffs of the Twin Buttes sometimes glowed in the sunset, and about the ever-present prairie wind and about the water tower and Wayne, whose grandfather had died recently, and about Jesse Walker, who let me drive his pickup, even though I didn't have a driver's license. And I told him that I wanted to become an author and write a book about him and Lilly because it was a story that only life itself could write. All this must have sounded childish to an old man, but I was mighty proud I was able to tell him the story of my life.

My shirt was sticking to my body, and I noticed some wet spots on JB's shirt. He loosened his tie and unbuttoned his collar, listening to me talk about Winstel and Mr. Ledbetter, who was worried about Hanna's future.

Sometimes he smiled, and sometimes he laughed, but he mostly remained serious, especially when I told him about my father and that I didn't know where he was. That seemed to worry him most. So I tried to tell him a few good things about dad, like that he had never hit me, ever. And that we had a terrible tumble with an old motorbike once, my father steering and me sitting in front on top of the tank, and that he carried me home for seven miles through the night and terrible weather. In the end, when I couldn't think of any other kind things to tell him about my father, he said, "You made up the motorbike story, didn't you?"

He could see through me. He understood that over time, I had invented a father because Jim Fletcher wasn't the one I wanted.

I didn't need to answer his question, nor did he have to ask again. From then on, I knew I couldn't fool him.

In the afternoon, we went to a small café, where he ordered coffee, and I ordered a Coke. We watched the people walking by outside — people who were in a hurry to get to someplace, and those who were strolling around as if they had no destination. Old people and young, men, women, and kids, a school class on their way to the museum on the other side of the street, a police officer who was talking to a young woman, and afterward, came inside to drink coffee and eat a doughnut. The TV was on, but I wasn't paying attention to it because I was under JB's spell. He told me about the day he and Lilly met for the first time and fell in love.

"When I gave her the rose, I was certain I'd see her

again. Only later, I had my doubts. I'd forgotten to give her my phone number or ask for hers. But how could I have in front of her parents? I could have gotten in trouble for leaving the room for blacks and walking over to the white people. All her father had to do was complain, and the cops would have been there in no time. The fear that I would never see Lilly again, it never left me. I tried to convince myself she'd come looking for me, that it would be easy to find her again because she was so beautiful, but doubt got the better of me, and finally, I ran all the way back to the restaurant. But she wasn't there anymore. The table where she had been sitting and the empty chair, a terrible sight. I checked whether she had left the rose behind, but it was gone. I asked the restaurant owner about her, but he didn't know her name, or whether she was from Baton Rouge. Nobody had seen her before. Wherever I asked, nobody knew anything about her. Months passed. I never gave up hope, though. I hoped she would one day stand in front of me because we were linked by our love, no matter how far our ways led us from each other. And then it happened." JB laughed. "One evening, when I was going to sing a song I'd written for her, called 'Lady in Blue,' for the first time, she was there…"

He broke off, leaned back and sipped his coffee.

"She walked into the club with Crazy Legs," I said.

The glow in his eyes faded.

"We don't want to talk about that, Bradley," he said. "You know, I made myself forget some things. At first, it wasn't easy. I was angry and wanted revenge. In Fort

Leavenworth, where they took me first, I wanted to break out. But I didn't manage to do that. I was helpless, and that made me even angrier."

"You took part in the prison riot."

"Yes, I was one of the ringleaders. We got news from the outside that people from the Klan had burned down the house I was born in, in Mississippi, not far from here. My father had built it for us. My sister got killed, and my mother."

"What happened?"

"Some people hated us because my father wasn't afraid to speak his mind, even when he got threatened. He was a strong man, but he wasn't there to protect his family when hooded riders came one moonless night and set fire to the house, while my mother and my sister were sleeping inside."

"And where was your father?"

"He'd been killed in town a year before when he took a cart of corn to the market. When I learned about the death of my mother and sister, I wanted to kill myself by busting my head against the cell wall. It didn't work. They put me in the prison hospital and patched me up again, but when it came to the first unrest, I wanted to be a part of it. I knew that if I were a ringleader, there was a good chance of being shot down by the guards or of being beaten to death. I didn't want to live anymore, not without Lilly."

"If you couldn't live without Lilly, why didn't you think of that before?"

"Before what?"

"Before you went to prison."

That puzzled him.

"Before you…" I paused, "before you killed that man."

He raised one eyebrow. I was afraid I had gone too far. I grabbed the Coke. My hand was trembling. He noticed and nodded.

"Yes, I remember that day well, Bradley," he said. "It turned out to be a very special day in both our lives, changing everything that was and everything we thought we could accomplish by staying together, a black man and a white woman. When I woke up, I asked Lilly if she wanted to be my wife. She was lying next to me and didn't move. I whispered the words into her ear and kissed her neck, and she woke up and asked me if it was just a dream or if I had asked her to be my wife. Well, I asked her again, and she said yes, and we stayed in bed all morning and made plans. We both knew it wouldn't be easy. We couldn't stay in Memphis. So we decided to move to Chicago. I had friends there. We went to the Peabody Hotel for lunch. In the afternoon, we drove down to the Mississippi and watched huge cotton bales get loaded. And we walked up to the Mississippi Bridge and looked down onto the river. And I guess it was like when you and Wayne are sitting on that water tower. You think about your life and about what's happened and about what you want for yourself, and you feel a kind of happiness, but at the same time, you fear losing it. I don't exactly know what Lilly was thinking when we were standing on the bridge and staring into the water, but I know part of her must have been thinking about what we would leave behind when we left Memphis. I sensed her sorrow. And I felt my own fear. All that day, it never let go of me. Except for the sat at that little table in Frank's Café. There, it dissolved like a lonely cloud in a blue sky. It was around five o'clock when we left the café. And then it happened. Lilly's told you about it."

"Tell me anyway."

"I've never told anybody."

"Why not?"

"Because nobody would have understood."

"Then tell me."

He leaned forward as if to prevent anyone from listening, but no one was near.

"I had bought the revolver - or the pistol as we called it back then - from a junk dealer named Perkins," he said. "I knew they would attack me one day. Lilly's father had threatened me more than once. Everybody knew it, the cops in the street, and the people at the club. Especially after the raid, when they arrested me. The police locked me up, and I thought they would hold me for twenty-four hours, but in the middle of the night, they pulled me out. Lilly's father was there with an attorney I knew was linked to the mob. And then, right in front of the grinning officers, Lilly's father told me that my days in Memphis were numbered. It was not a warning. It was a threat. He was prepared to pay someone to kill me, which was as much as I understood. I turned to the cops and asked if they had heard him threaten me with death, but they just grinned and said I should think fast about getting myself a dark-skinned girlfriend and keep my fingers off fair maidens. From then on, I took the pistol wherever I went, even when Lilly was with me. When we came out of Frank's Café, I knew what would happen. Lilly was unaware of the danger. I never told her about her father's threats. She didn't realize I'd been in fear for my life for weeks. Nobody knew.

I saw three or four cops close by when we left Frank's Café, but I knew they weren't there to protect us. I didn't know the men who were waiting for me. I'd only seen one of them before that day, a black man named Lawrence. I didn't know him, but I'd seen him with Crazy Legs and a few other guys who hung around the back rooms of the Royal Blue. All of them were gangsters. I despised them for what they were and for what they were prepared to do on behalf of others."

I remembered what the street sweeper had told me; that the men started to push JB around, and that he told them he wanted to walk on in peace. But they wouldn't let him go.

Now JB sat in front of me, half a century between that day and this, but in his eyes, I could see the grief it caused him to call up these memories.

"They insulted me in a way I couldn't counter because Lilly was with me. I told them to leave us alone. They laughed at me. Then they started insulting Lilly. I warned them. To no avail. Then I punched Lawrence in the face. I wanted to walk on, but all of a sudden, one of them had a baseball bat in his hands and hit me. Three of them pulled Lilly across the street, and Lawrence kicked me in the face. I tried to defend myself, but the one with the bat hit me on the arm. 'Next time, we crush your skull, nigger,' he said, while I knelt on the ground. And then he said something else. It was the reason I pulled the pistol out of my pocket and pulled the trigger."

I looked at him, wondering. "They claimed you shot him as he walked away."

"Everything happened very quickly, Bradley. From the moment I grabbed the pistol to the moment, he dropped to the ground only a few seconds passed."

"What did he say to you?"

He avoided my eyes. "You don't want to know, Bradley."

"Tell me anyway!"

He remained silent for a long time. Then he raised his head. "Don't ask me about it again."

That was that. It was late afternoon, and I could tell JB was tired. His eyes were red, and his shoulders were sagging. He wanted to go back to the prison he called his home. And he wanted to be left alone.

He said he had to go, then got up and left. I watched him as he walked to the door, not as upright and straight as he'd been that morning, but like a man on the last stretch of his life, someone who needs some peace before setting out on a new road.

I almost ran after him, but I remained seated, with the empty Coke glass on the table in front of me.

He stopped at the door as if deciding whether to leave or turn around. Turn around, I urged him in my mind. And that's what he did.

"You know what makes me mad, Bradley?" he shouted

over to me.

I shrugged. "What?"

"That scoundrel hung my guitar on his wall."

He opened the door and shuffled out, an old man tired out by remembering.

Nothing extraordinary had happened that day, but still, I was confident JB would return to Memphis with me. Maybe in a roundabout way, but in the end, he'd get there, where Lilly was waiting for him.

CHAPTER 19
BACK TO THE BEGINNING

The urn that holds Lilly's ashes sits on a shelf in my room. I'm sitting at my writing desk by the window trying to play "Lady in Blue" on JB's guitar, humming along with it. Through the open window, I can see the Rimrocks glowing in the distance. This light makes the contours softer, almost liquid, and the distant chain of hills don't look like the body of a naked woman reclining anymore, but rather, like a glowing stream of blood between heaven and earth. The wind has been tearing through Winstel all day, so dust is hanging in the air, and the sun is a pale ball right above the horizon. I lay the guitar on my bed and lean back in my chair. I'm thinking about going downstairs to the café for a Coke. The letter from Hanna sits unopened in front of me on the old typewriter, which I rarely use anymore. I have a computer now, and it produces a low sound that reminds me of the noise the air conditioning made in my small room at the motel in Hattiesburg where I spent a sleepless night waiting for the next day.

The air conditioning wasn't working right. I kept turning the control knob, but nothing happened. The cold air coming through smelled awful. I switched the air conditioning off. Within a few minutes, I was covered in sweat. So I switched it on again and tried to go to sleep. It was impossible. I turned on the television. One of the channels was showing a movie starring Nicole Kidman. I liked Nicole Kidman. Her eyes reminded me of Lilly's eyes. Clear as glass. You could see everything in them. Hatred, anger, disappointment, mourning, love. Everything.

After midnight, I wrote a letter to Hanna, which, in the morning, I flushed down the toilet. I grabbed my duffel bag and left the room. It had been drizzling overnight, and the air was sticky. I walked to the nearest payphone and dialed the number my father had given me the last time. A recording said the phone number was no longer in use. I called home. Mitch was there and gave me hell because it was only half past five.

"Tell mom everything's fine," I said.

"Where are you?"

"In Hattiesburg."

"Where the hell is that?"

"Mississippi," I said and hung up. I walked down the street as far as the next doughnut shop, where I had a Coke and two doughnuts, one with vanilla cream filling, the other a cream puff.

It was eight o'clock when I arrived at Forrest County Jail. The officer from the day before sat at the reception desk. She beamed as if she'd been expecting me.

I wanted to sit down on the bench, but the door opened, and JB entered the room. He was dressed exactly as the day before, without the tie. But his shirt was done up to the last button. I immediately noticed the small suitcase in his hand. He approached and stopped in front of me. For a few seconds, we looked into each other's eyes, and then he nodded and said, "Come on, Bradley. Let's go."

My eyes began to burn when we left Forrest County

Jail. I quickly wiped the tears with the back of my hand, but I don't think JB would have noticed anyway.

We didn't go far. JB wanted to visit the bank where he had deposited the money he'd been earning as a janitor. He didn't know how much it was, but he withdrew a thousand dollars.

"How do you want the money, Mr. Swift?" the teller asked.

"In an envelope," JB said.

The man smiled, got the amount out in big and small bills, which he then counted out slowly.

JB put the larger notes in the envelope to carry in the outside pocket of his suitcase, and the rest he put into his wallet.

"Where do you want to go?" I asked him as we left the bank. He stopped on the stairs and took a deep breath. It felt as if we'd just made the long and steep ascent to the top of the Twin Buttes, and the whole world lay spread out below us, or at least what had been my world until then.

I saw as far as South Wichita, noticing the small spots in the shimmering heat that were Winstel, the dead-straight road to Dickens. And if I looked very carefully, I saw the blood on the naked rock where Santiago Gomez had died.

"Where are we going?" I asked again.

"Baton Rouge," he replied. "Everything began there."

"Baton Rouge, here we come!" I said, laughing. "Maybe we'll find your guitar."

We walked down the stairs and to the Greyhound

station, bought two tickets to Baton Rouge, and waited for the next bus.

The journey didn't take long. JB had the window seat and was staring outside as if there were more to look at out there than what I could see. Forests, rivers, lakes, calm waters, which weren't flowing anywhere, moss hanging from the branches of huge old trees, houses with gabled roofs, most of them painted white, side streets with cars giving way to buses, schools, playgrounds, churches, warehouses, factories, gas stations. Hardly any people. Somewhere, a little boy was pulling on the collar of his dog. In front of a small church, people clad in dark clothing were standing and talking while a coffin was being carried down the stairs. The bus stopped, and somebody got on — a man with a sickening smell. For a long time, I couldn't figure out where the odor was coming from, even though it was familiar. It smelled like the old car tires behind Jesse Walker's shed.

JB saw all that. And more. I don't believe anything on this trip escaped him. I would have liked to have asked him because I wanted to see the world through his eyes, but I left him in peace until he put the question to me.

"Bradley, does Lilly know you found me?"

"No, I haven't called her. I've thought about calling her, but figured she would get too worked up if I did."

"Tell me more about her," he said.

"What should I tell you, Grandfather?"

It was the first time I'd called him that. He didn't react but told me to tell him everything, whatever came to my mind. How Lilly was doing in the old folks' home with all the other old folks. I told him about my first visit with my father, and about the old men and women who stole cake from each other's plates. And I told him about the photo Lilly had put up in her small room, about the bench in the garden, and about the sunlight, through which she remembered everything that used to be.

JB listened, without interrupting me once. At some point, his chin fell onto his chest, and he seemed to doze off, but every time the bus jerked, he opened his eyes.

I told him about my last visit with Lilly and that she was probably waiting for news from me, but I stopped telling him stories when I saw a sign announcing the town of Baton Rouge fly by, and the city' skyline appear in front of us.

It was noon when we stopped at the large parking lot in front of the bus station. We were getting ready to get off the bus when one of the other passengers, a dark-skinned man with gray hair, held JB back by his arm.

"Sorry, Mister, but I believe I know you."

"I don't think so," JB replied.

"Then you aren't JB Swift, the one they used to call The Legend?"

"No."

The man apologized one more time.

Later, when we were in the taxi, I asked JB why he had lied.

JB shrugged. He didn't say anything for a long time. Then I heard him sigh.

"You're right, Bradley. Why shouldn't I have told him? I've been dead for too long. I need to get used to the idea of being alive again."

We drove down the street where the restaurant had been, the one where JB had seen Lilly for the first time. It wasn't there anymore. Only the façade with the two entrances was still the same, with one door leading into a Korean grocery store, the other into a Chinese restaurant. JB and I stood in front of the house for a long time and looked at the old plaster, with scraps of paper clinging on in some places, which, once upon a time, formed part of a colorful poster. JB seemed to be comparing everything he saw to what was left in his memory.

"This used to be the bar and a small diner," he said, pointing to the entrance of the grocery store. "With a sign on the wall next to the door that said Negroes only."

"Let's go inside," I said.

He hesitated, but then followed me. Once inside I noticed right away that the restaurant where Lilly and her parents had dinner and the bar where JB had sat at a table with his friends were separated now by a solid wall without a sliding door. The owner was in the process of hanging dead geese in the window. When we entered, he wiped his hands on a cloth, made the cloth disappear, and positioned himself behind the counter.

"How can I help you?" he asked politely. I told him why we were there, but my story didn't mean anything to him. He explained that he had taken the store over three years earlier. He believed the counter had been a bar counter once, which then was lowered and given a new top. JB stared at the separating wall behind a shelf stacked with cans and other containers. I was sure he could see Lilly through the wall, Lilly with her father and her mother, the light on her hair, her beautiful face, and how she quickly lowered her head when she could feel he was looking at her.

I thanked the Korean grocer, and we went to the restaurant next door. I told the owner the same story, and she smiled. JB pointed to a round table near the window.

"Lilly was sitting there," he said. "At that table."

"A wonderful memory," the owner responded.

"Yes! So wonderful it hurts."

I didn't know whether the owner comprehended everything we said, but she understood what JB meant. The memory could be so beautiful that the thought of never returning could almost break your heart.

Where Crazy Legs' Dance Club once stood, there was a new building made of cement and glass, which belonged to an insurance company. At the street corner was a newsstand. I asked the vendor, a man with a glass eye that stared past me, whether anyone was left in the area who remembered the old dance club. The man referred us to a shoe shiner named Pete "White Shoe" Bowles, who had his stand on the corner of 9th Street and Choctaw Drive, where there was a small municipal park.

"I think back then, shortly before the house with the dance bar burned down, Pete was the business partner of a man who called himself Crazy Legs."

We walked to the park on foot. The shoe shiner was probably a few years younger than JB. His short beard was salt and pepper. He was wearing white shoes, flimsy trousers, a Hawaiian shirt, a vest, and a derby hat.

When he saw us coming, he glanced at our shoes. While he had nothing but a scornful twitch in the corner of his mouth for my dusty cowboy boots, JB's brown shoes, with their elaborate stitching, produced an appreciative nod.

"Wonderful shoes, sir," he said. "Such exquisite work one sees less and less these days. Allow me to ask you, sir, where you bought them? Not here in Baton Rouge, I would guess?"

"At Saul T. Lyons in South Lauderdale Street, diagonally opposite Dino's Ice-Cream Parlor."

"Memphis!" The shoe shiner blurted out, after having thought about it for two or three seconds. "Between Carter's bookshop and the pharmacy. Before the war. JB Swift was the main..." The shoe shiner's eyes almost popped out of his head. He reached into his vest pocket, fished out small, metal-rimmed glasses and placed them on top of his nose, which had a striking similarity to a wrinkled plum. He looked at JB as if he were standing before a monument. "God strike me down. There he is in front of me, alive, in the flesh, as if he had risen from the dead. You'll have to explain that to me."

"My grandson here, Bradley Fletcher, got me out of Hattiesburg prison," JB said, not without pride in his voice.

"Out of Hattiesburg prison? Why on earth did I think you were six feet under long ago, looking up at the daisies? That must be one of those miracles that nobody can explain. Sit down, JB Swift, and let me give your beautiful shoes a mirror polish."

"I would have to be a yellow-bellied nigger to let my shoes be shined by somebody who did business with Crazy Legs," JB said.

Yellow-bellied. I had never heard the term before in my life. Not in Winstel. An equivalent word would be coward or something like that. But White Shoe got the picture right away.

"I already guessed there was a reason for your coming here," he answered. "Yes, I was the partner of a scoundrel, a man called Crazy Legs, and I curse the day I met him. The dance hall, which I had put all my savings in, burned down. The insurance paid for the damage. It was a small fortune, and the cheating bastard ran off with it before I could hang him from his tie, which I would no doubt have done, in the state of mind I was. So when you talk to me, you are not talking to a yellow-bellied nigger, but to a man who got cheated out of the fruits of his labor. But I don't want to whine. I've known better times. People used to know who Pete 'White Shoe' Bowles was. I performed in New Orleans and Memphis and Kansas City."

"Sorry, but the name doesn't ring a bell."

"It was after your time when I came to Memphis," explained White Shoe. "I regret that. When I was young, I wished for nothing more than to be there at one of your gigs. I was the proud owner of one of your records. Bayou Baby. I never had the luck to make a record myself, but I played with several people with whose names you should be familiar. In the end, shortly before I bought into the dancehall business, I played the bass, even for B.B. King. And then, unfortunately, I was taken in by that scoundrel in this town."

"That scoundrel has cheated you out of your savings and me out of a bundle of years of my life."

"I'd heard what happened in Memphis back there, but didn't have a clue that the scoundrel, whose name I don't want to speak out loud anymore, even if it's just a nickname, had anything to do with it." With a gesture, he asked JB to take a seat on the chair, and, this time, JB accepted his invitation.

"It's an honor," he said, putting his small suitcase onto the pavement and climbing onto the dark red upholstered chair mounted on the platform. Carefully, he pulled up his trouser legs a little, and the white socks became visible. White Shoe took two brushes out of his case, rubbed the bristles against one another quickly, and began to clean JB's shoes.

"Mr. Swift, I hope you and this young cowboy didn't come to Baton Rouge on the assumption that you would find him here."

"My grandson, Bradley Fletcher, is from Texas," said JB, as if he believed he had to protect me and my cowboy boots. "Of course, I'd like to find out if this scoundrel, as you call him, is still to be found anywhere, but we've come to Baton Rouge mainly to look for my guitar."

I felt this to be my cue, and I pulled the photo out of my duffel bag and held it under White Shoe's nose. He looked at it through his spectacles.

"This guitar here," I said, pointing at it. "It belongs to my grandfather. We would like to know what happened to it."

"As far as I know, it wasn't hanging on the wall anymore when the dance hall burned down. I think the rascal sold the guitar and other instruments from his collection to a man named William Ogden shortly before he set the fire, which, of course, could never be proven."

"And who is this William Ogden?" I asked.

"He deals in old weapons and other junk."

"Here in Baton Rouge?"

"He owns an antique shop not far from here. His house, a grand mansion from before the Civil War, is located on Bayou Duplantier, south of town."

"I guess it wouldn't be a simple thing to visit Mr. Ogden and ask him about the guitar," JB said.

"Mr. Ogden leads a retired life. His property is said to be guarded by a pack of dogs. His son Benedict runs his businesses. Once in a while, I see his car drive by."

"And where is the antique shop?"

"W.J. Ogden & Son is located on the corner of Government and Third Street. That's downtown."

"And you wouldn't know Crazy Legs' whereabouts by any chance, would you?" JB asked.

"He's roasting in hell, I hope, but sometimes, I fear that he could even have succeeded in cheating God. Every night, before I fall asleep, I wish the everlasting plague on him."

"A wish I readily share with you, Mr. Bowles."

Pete "White Shoe" Bowles put a nice-smelling cream

on JB's shoes. Then he began to shine them with a soft cloth and gave them a mirror polish.

When JB wanted to pay him for his work, he declined by saying that it had been an extraordinary honor to serve a living Legend of the blues. But he insisted on JB signing his name in his client book, where hundreds of more or less famous persons had already left their autographs. JB wrote his and also my name in the book. And underneath, he wrote, "For Mr. Pete 'White Shoe' Bowles. One day, we'll play the blues together, my friend."

It wasn't an easy goodbye, but I consoled myself with the thought that the dedication JB had written in the shoe shiner's book, perhaps, was some sort of a prophecy and that we would all see each other again.

WERNER J. EGLI

CHAPTER 20
JB'S GUITAR

W.J. Ogden & Son's antique shop was in a yellow building dating back to the past century, squeezed between two large glass boxes. The building on the left was a bank, and the one on the right was a bookstore that looked like a bank.

We found JB's guitar in the shop as if it had been kept there for him. It stood in a glass cabinet, illuminated by a small, hidden lamp. We both saw it immediately as we entered, and I was about to walk right up to it when JB stopped short as if he didn't dare go near the old guitar. It had been fifty years since he last held it in his hands.

The shop was a hall with a marble floor and whitewashed walls. A crystal chandelier hung from the ceiling on three heavy golden chains. Wall lights illuminated oil paintings in gilded frames. I assumed that they all had been painted by world-famous artists. Bronze sculptures, old clocks, and vases stood on marble pillars. Underneath my cowboy boots, a rug spread out on the shining floor. It probably once had hung in the palace of an Arabian oil sheik and had been woven by hand from silk and goat hair. I was just about to take a step forward and move off the rug when a door opened between two marble pillars.

A young man with a reddish face, blue eyes, and yellow, orange hair entered the shop. Tall he was, with small hands and a little mouth. He couldn't have been older than twenty-five, and he wore a black, custom-made suit and black shoes, which sparkled almost as much as JB's did. The man gave us the once-over and quickly concluded that we got ourselves lost. The fact that I had dared tread on his rug with my Texan shitkickers prevented him from asking how he could help us. Instead, he said, "I assume you walked in the wrong door, folks."

I found myself wishing I had stepped in dog crap outside before entering the store. I let my duffel bag slide off my shoulders and flop onto the rug.

"We're where we exactly wanted to be," JB said to the man and set his suitcase on the floor. "Someone told us that this shop belongs to a man called W.J. Ogden. It's him we wish to speak to."

The left corner of the man's mouth twitched. But there was no room for a smile in this snob's face, with its ridiculous little mustache.

He took two steps toward us.

"Mr. William Ogden, who is my father, retired almost a year ago. My name is Benedict Ogden. Please tell me what you want, and please make it quick. I'm busy."

"My name is Swift," JB said. "This here is my grandson Bradley. He's from Texas, and he got me out of Forrest County Jail in Hattiesburg today."

The young man went a shade paler. He most likely feared for his life. Those two steps he had taken toward us, well, he took them back.

"Mr. Swift, what do you want from my father or me?"

JB pointed to the guitar in the glass cabinet. "It belongs to me," he said.

Benedict Ogden opened his mouth and forgot to shut it. He walked to the cabinet and positioned himself next to it.

"This guitar is a masterpiece of an instrument, a real Morrison blues guitar, which got famous before World War II, probably in the thirties. Before Cyrus Morrison got famous, that is and was able to afford employees. In other words, he built it himself. And it's for a left-handed person. That is an especially valuable instrument because it has Cyrus Morrison's initials on it." Ogden took a deep breath. "Allow me to assume that neither you nor your young companion from Texas can come up with the money needed to purchase this exquisite piece of art."

"You are correct," JB said and laughed out loud. "And how much is this guitar supposed to cost?"

"An acceptable price would almost certainly be above twenty thousand dollars. However, this guitar is not for sale, because it forms part of my father's collection of rare musical instruments. I've borrowed it as a central piece for our small exhibition."

"Twenty thousand dollars," JB said, shaking his head. "That's a princely sum for my old Ham, especially when it can only be played left-handed. Would you allow me to hold it?"

Ogden looked at JB in amazement and with pity.

"Unfortunately, that's not possible, my friend. As you can see, the cabinet is locked."

"Then go get the key."

"Why should I do that? I've already told you this

musical instrument is an exhibition piece." The snob glanced at his gold watch. "Would you excuse me?" He walked to the shop door and opened it as if he wanted to let in fresh air. Neither JB nor I made a move to honor this silent request to leave the shop.

"Would you please go now?" Benedict Ogden finally brought himself to say. "This guitar is not for sale and — "

"I don't think I will leave this store without my guitar," JB interrupted him. "Your father bought it from a con man, whose name I don't want to say out loud. This scoundrel stole it many years ago."

Ogden apparently didn't want to believe what he was hearing.

"If you don't get out, I'll have no choice but to call the police!"

"You'd better call your father and tell him I've come to collect my guitar. I'm pretty sure he knows its stolen property."

Ogden leaned out the door and shouted to a passerby that he was being held up in his shop and that the police should get called. Instead of calling the cops, the man quickened his pace and hurried across the street.

"Show him the photo in the book," JB said to me. I bent down to open the duffel bag and show him the picture, but Ogden seemed to think I wanted to pull a weapon on him. He freaked out, running into the street screaming for help, pointing to the shop door, which closed automatically.

It took less than three minutes for the police to arrive.

Three patrol cars, sirens wailing and blue lights flashing. Six men, weapons ready. Two of them approached the shop door. Through the window, I could see two of the others take cover behind a concrete bench and a hydrant. The remaining two stopped the traffic and the pedestrians.

The two cops racing for the shop door were holding onto their pistols with both hands. Everything was acted like in a scene of a movie. Arriving at the door, one of them moved to the outside corner by the window. The other one pushed open the door with his shoulder, jumped inside, and immediately started to scream at us.

JB had put up his hands a long time ago, and I had followed his example, assuming that he had experience with situations of this kind.

"On your bellies, you damn dogs!" the first cop yelled at us, while the others rushed in shouting and screaming.

"Come on! Get down, you assholes! I'm counting to three; then you're on your bellies! One, two..."

I went down on my knees and threw myself onto my belly.

"The same applies to you, nigger!" one shouted at JB, who had more trouble kneeling and lying face down with his hands raised.

When we both were lying next to each other, JB panting on the cold marble floor due to the strain, me on the Oriental rug. I noticed JB's nose was bleeding. Two more cops stormed into the shop. One of them, who I couldn't see, kicked me in the side. Another shouted at me to put my hands on my back. I did. But somebody pushed cold steel into my neck anyway, presumably the muzzle of his pistol. The handcuffs clicked, and I got grabbed by a fist and thrown about so that I ended up lying on the rug on my side.

"Do you have a name, punk?" one of the cops barked at me.

"Bradley Fletcher," I gasped. "The old man is my grandfather."

"Stand up!"

They pulled us both to our feet. JB was still bleeding from his nose. Meanwhile, Benedict Ogden had come into the shop, arrogant as someone used to like nobody else but himself.

"I had warned those two," he explained to the cops. "The old one claims the young one got him out of jail, Forrest County Jail in Hattiesburg."

"Hattiesburg?" A young black cop laughed out loud. "I had a hunch straight away that I knew you, Grandpa. You're the janitor there in Hattiesburg, aren't you? Your name's JB Swift, right? In the old days, they called you The Legend."

"That's me," JB said. "And the young man here is my grandson Bradley. From Texas. We've come here to fetch my guitar."

"Your guitar?" the cop asked.

Ogden pointed over to the glass cabinet. "He says he used to own the guitar there."

For some minutes, the cops forgot they'd arrested us. They were looking at the guitar.

"An ancient Morrison blues guitar," Ogden explained.

"Probably built by Cyrus Morrison himself. It's part of my father's collection."

"It's him we want to talk to," I said quickly. "And in case nobody believes us, I have a photograph of this guitar in my duffel bag."

"If I remember correctly, you've spent the last fifty years or so in jail, Mr. Swift," said the cop who knew JB. "I don't know what makes you think this old guitar could still be your property today when it belongs to Mr. Ogden's collection."

"Mr. Ogden bought it off a con man some years ago."

"Of whom?" the young Ogden asked scornfully. "He doesn't want to speak the name."

"Crazy Legs," I snapped, "he owned a dance club here in Baton Rouge, the one that burned down some years ago. Pete Bowles, the shoe shiner, told us that it was possible this crook conned the insurance company by putting the guitar on the list of lost items."

"White Shoe Bowles?" asked one of the other cops. "Wasn't he the partner of — "

"He was also deceived, and cheated out of all his savings," I interrupted the cop. "We've come here to negotiate with Mr. William J. Ogden over the guitar, and we still want to do that. That's why it would be appropriate if somebody could take these handcuffs off of us."

"They both belong in jail!" Ogden claimed, but one of the cops explained to him that there was indeed no reason to arrest us.

"On the contrary, Mr. Ogden, severe accusations are

being made against you and your father. I'm sure you are familiar with our laws. A person in possession of stolen property — "

"That's a ridiculous accusation!" Ogden shouted. "Where would we be if we paid attention to what any Tom, Dick, or Jack says, for Christ's sake? The law…"

"Mr. Ogden," one of the cops cut him short, "maybe you would like to ask your father about the origin of this guitar."

"Then let me just talk to him for a minute. I'm sure he's able to prove where the guitar comes from."

The cops let him disappear into the office. As he had left the door open, we could all hear him, all but JB perhaps, who had lost some of his hearing.

Ogden misdialed the first time. We could hear him cursing and dialing again. Then he had his father on the line, who he didn't call father, but sir.

"There are some problems, sir. An old man and a young fellow from Texas are in the shop and maintain that the Cyrus Morrison guitar in the glass cabinet is stolen property."

Silence. And then: "The old man's name? Swift or something like that. JB Swift. More than fifty years ago, the guitar was supposed to have been — "

He stopped in the middle of the sentence.

"You're coming here, sir? Now? Okay, sir, I will — "

Ogden swallowed the rest of the words. The cops exchanged looks. It took almost half a minute before Ogden reappeared, with quite a few reddish blotches on his face and looking hounded in his eyes.

"I guess you can take off their handcuffs now. My father is on his way."

After the cops took off the handcuffs, Ogden went into the office again and came back with the key to the cabinet and tissue he handed to JB to wipe his bloody nose. Then, without saying a word, he walked to the cabinet and opened it. Carefully he took out the old guitar, looked at it for a long while before turning to JB and handing it to him.

JB nodded briefly, quickly checked the back of the guitar, smiling when he saw his initials still on it. He sat down on one of the antique chairs, holding his old guitar. We all looked at him, wanted him to do something, to play it or at least touch the strings, but he just sat there smiling with his guitar on his lap.

CHAPTER 21
LAUGH, CLOWN, LAUGH

JB gave the guitar to me before he died. Sometimes when I have writer's block, I hold it. I'm not a good player, but this guitar comes to life in my hands. As if JB gave me a sense of music with it, which he had inherited from his ancestors. Sometimes I play for hours, twanging melodies I've never heard before, as well as those JB used to sing with his husky voice, just for Lilly, until he died.

I don't know any blues musician who could handle lyrics and melodies the way JB did. Albert King, maybe. Perhaps Sleepy John Estes. I've had their records in my collection for a long time, ancient vinyl records by Frank Stokes and Noah Lewis. Gus Cannon and Will Batts and Memphis Minnie. I know them all. And I also like Stevie Ray Vaughn, even though he belonged to the new generation and was white, and from Texas. A few days ago, I bought *Lie to Me*, the CD by Johnny Lang, at Winstel's General Store. I'm sure if JB were still alive, he'd say this boy had the blues in his blood like nobody else.

I have to thank William J. Ogden for owning JB's guitar in the first place. He wouldn't have had to give it to us. That's what the cops said. JB couldn't raise a legitimate claim on the guitar. The two initials JB had carefully carved into the wood also made no difference. The masterpiece by Cyrus Morrison got publicly auctioned off after JB went to prison. But, no documentation relating to this sale had survived, and no one knew who first took possession of the guitar. That meant Mr. William J. Ogden was the rightful owner of the guitar, which he had bought from Bukka "Crazy Legs" Harris a few months before the dance hall burned down.

I never saw Ogden again and don't know if he's still alive. Though not very tall, he made a tremendous impression on me when he entered the antique store that day.

He was wearing simple clothes. Light linen trousers flapped around his legs. He wore sandals, and his shirt hung low. Nothing about him would have given away the fact that he was one of the wealthiest men in Baton Rouge, but I believe he was capable of moving mountains.

"JB Swift," was all he said when he entered, and he had the radiant smile of a child. With his hand stretched out, he walked toward JB, who was still sitting with the guitar on his knees.

JB got up holding his guitar with his left hand by its neck and shook hands. "I saw you in Memphis," Ogden said, holding on to JB's hand. "You performed with Ray Hart and Willie Boy Taylor. I think you were on your way back from Chicago, where you had recorded your first album. Later I went to Kansas City to see you play again. I saw you one more time, at the Royal Blue. That was a few weeks before the accident. You cannot imagine what this handshake means to me."

"In those days, I made music for the colored people, Mr. Ogden," JB said hesitantly. "White people came to the Royal Blue only on rare occasions."

"I was one of the few," replied Mr. Ogden and laughed. "How did we put it in those days? One night on Beale Street and a white person don't want to be white anymore. That applied to me. I liked the music. It made me feel alive, and I wanted to live. Believe me, when you sang your song 'Lady in Blue' in honor of a breathtaking young lady, I was sitting at one of the tables with the girl I later married. Her name was Mary Jane. She was studying at the University of Memphis with her friend Sue and the young lady we called JB's girl after that evening when she came to the Royal Blue for the first time."

I looked at JB's face from the side, and even though nobody else would have noticed it, I realized he was agitated. I had only known him since the day before and, of course, I wasn't able to tell what was happening inside him. However, I think the memories of that night in the Royal Blue revived a longing that had been buried deep inside him for fifty years.

"Lilly," he said quietly, but in a way, everyone in the room could understand. "Her name was Lilly."

"Yes, I know. Mary Jane told me about her now and then. You know, we tried to help Lilly out after the judgment was pronounced, but she rejected any help. In those days, I was a young attorney without money and influence. Otherwise, I would have tried to appeal against this disgraceful judgment. But then the war broke out. And later, after the prison riot at Leavenworth, unfortunately, it wasn't possible anymore."

Finally, Ogden let go of JB's hand and turned to me.

"I assume you are his grandson and your grandmother is that beautiful lady from the Royal Blue who made my heart beat faster, even though I realized that hers would only beat for one man, for JB Swift."

He held out his hand to me.

"I'm Bradley," I said.

"I was hoping for a son from Mary Jane, a son like you. It wasn't to be. Mary Jane died when she was thirty-five years old, from cancer. I married again. Benedict came from that marriage."

He turned around to face his son.

"Benedict, I've kept this guitar for a man without knowing if he would ever come to claim it. But I've been hoping he would all these years."

"Why have you never told me, sir?" young Ogden asked. "All I knew was that this guitar wasn't for sale."

"You didn't need to know more," Ogden smiled. I felt sorry for the little snob. Mr. Ogden dismissed the two cops and invited us to stay with him in his home. I think he was a lonely man, even though he had a family and a pack of Rottweilers guarding his estate.

Never in my life had I seen a home like Mr. Ogden's, let alone spent the night in one. The houses in Winstel were all small, except Hanna's. But in comparison to William J. Ogden's mansion, the Ledbetter's villa was nothing to write home about. This palace had been built in a time when the area around Bayou Duplantier was a vast plantation with hundreds of black slaves working the fields. Like a palace from ancient Greece, it stood in the middle of what seemed like a park, in the shade of the largest trees I'd ever seen. Eight columns built from brick, plastered over and covered in marble painting, carried the roof over the porch. The main house was a two-story structure with two single-story wings. We took the stairs up to the porch, where a small table and two wickers stood.

Mrs. Ogden, Benedict's mother, was a petite woman, some twenty, or even thirty, years younger than her husband. She appeared reserved and seemed to have neither the inclination nor the time to entertain us. When Ogden suggested we should all look at the collection of instruments in the west wing, she said she had an appointment that couldn't be put off. And then she disappeared, and we didn't see her until sunset.

Mr. Ogden's collection consisted of instruments by American makers and musicians. He even owned one of the guitars that the most famous of all country musicians, Hank Williams, had with him when he died in the back seat of a limousine on his way to a concert. And a violin that the legendary Powers Thornton had played. There were instruments of the Bynum and Jim Turner Band, one of the first bands to play the blues on Beale Street, as well as homemade instruments of the Cajuns of the Mississippi Delta.

JB and Mr. Ogden spent almost the entire day talking about the old days and the history of the blues, which, by then, I was starting to know about more and more. But I kept my mouth shut, letting myself be carried off by their nostalgia, back to 1913, when Dark Town Follies hit the stage, a play written by J. Lubrie Hill. Then to

1927, when Little Charley Holmes was the top attraction of the great Robert Henry Band, with the song "Laugh, Clown, Laugh." And then was famous W.C. Handy, the father of Beale Street.

A few years later, in the forties and fifties, B.B. King and Albert King and the other big men of the blues, all performed in Memphis at one time or another, on Beale Street, where JB also later became a legend. They were both indulging in their memories, but when Mr. Ogden asked him to play a piece on his guitar, JB refused.

"The first time I'll be playing again, it will be for Lilly," he said.

Mr. Ogden understood, and my heart almost burst. I was confident he would be returning to Memphis with me.

In the evening, when the blood-red sun shone through the massive trees and made the Spanish moss glow, Ogden put an old RCA record on his gramophone. I admired how the thing turned, and the needle ate into the grooves. Scratchy sounds emerged then all of a sudden the music set in with a singing voice I had never heard but recognized nonetheless. It was JB Swift performing "Lady in Blue" accompanied by a small orchestra. The mood turned festive, with the sunset and the blues that JB had sung for the first time in public at the Royal Blue, for Lilly and her alone.

Later, at dinner, we talked about the music of today and the blues and naturally, Mrs. Ogden, who had come home in the evening, asked what had happened on Beale Street that day, but JB merely said he didn't want to think about it.

I asked myself if he was about to put the past behind him, now that he finally had a future.

After dinner, we sat outside on the porch for a while, and someone let the dogs out of their enclosure; soon they had all come to us to get be petted.

"Don't be fooled," Mrs. Ogden warned. "They aren't as harmless as they pretend to be."

JB and I spent the night in two rooms in the east wing; both were at least three times as high as my room in Winstel. Plaster Stucco covered the ceiling and the walls. There was an oil painting, which showed an ocean bay, and another of a man in a Confederate major's uniform. Even though the walls of the house were quite thick, I couldn't go to sleep for a long time, because JB was strumming away on his guitar next door, quietly and cautiously it seemed, but I was able to hear every single note the guitar produced as I pressed my ear against the wall, and sometimes even held my breath so not a single note would escape me. Then there was silence. At least for the few minutes before JB started to snore loudly. Again, there was no chance of going to sleep. I thought about Lilly. She slept quietly. On several occasions, she had fallen asleep while I was sitting and playing a card game with her, a game she called "Bolivia." It made no difference to her whether she was winning or losing. At some point, she leaned back into the cushions, sighed, and fell asleep. I usually stayed with her and watched how her face became smooth in her sleep. Every time, I wished I could meet her at that very moment in her dream. Her zest for life must have made her attractive back then. How had she appeared to Mr. Ogden when she came to the Royal Blue for the first time? Breathtaking, was how he described her.

All those years JB and Lilly had lived — as if being together had just been a dream. They'd been made for each other back then, but now they both had their peculiarities and their new fears. A lot could change in fifty years.

I had no idea what would happen in Memphis if they met again. For the third time. Would it be the last? Would they spend the rest of their lives together?

I wasn't able to control my anxiety as I lay sleepless in bed. At some point, however, I dropped off and slept so soundly that it took me a while to realize where I was when I woke the next morning.

We left the Ogden's home after a delicious breakfast. A driver took us down to the Greyhound Station in a limousine, where people looked at us incredulously as we got out, walked to the counter, and bought two tickets to Memphis.

When I tried to call Lilly, Rhonda told me she was at the hairdresser's and would be back around noon.

"She wasn't there," I said to JB. "She's at the hairdresser's."

"At the hairdresser's?"

"Yes. Lilly is making herself pretty for you."

He grinned. "Then she must know we're coming."

I nodded. "Lilly knows."

CHAPTER 22
THE MIRACLE OF LOVE

The journey from Baton Rouge to Memphis seemed endless. I could hardly wait to see Lilly again. We were supposed to arrive sometime in the afternoon. All morning, we rode northward along the eastern bank of the Mississippi, through the bayous and their extensive woodlands and meadows, with the old plantations and the small villages, where the blacks outnumbered the whites. The first stop along our way was Natchez; then, we traveled a stretch along the Trace, still northbound, but rarely came close enough to the Mississippi actually to see it.

JB called this mighty river The Old Man, and I knew it well after being there on the raft with Tom Sawyer, Huck Finn and Indian Joe in Mark Twain's books, which I had discovered in a box in the attic of our house in Winstel. They had belonged to my father when he was a boy, and they must have meant a lot to him, as there wasn't much else he kept from his youth.

I thought of dad while we drove north, wondering where he might be now; perhaps he was driving his truck somewhere, or lying in bed with some woman, somewhere in Montana or Idaho, or maybe it was California again.

He knew no peace — no place in the world he would have wanted to stay for any length of time. I didn't even know if he was looking for such a place or if he simply had no destination. Men, who always leave, yet never arrive anywhere.

"One day, he'll find peace," mom had told us once. "He can't go on like this forever. For some people, it just takes a bit longer to find it."

I wished I could have called him, or at least had an address I could have sent a letter. My notebook contained ten phone numbers I had crossed out, over ten names of women I had already forgotten. He called my mother, Dove. Little Dove, when he was in a good mood. For a while, he called me Champ. I hated it, and he noticed and called me Brad from then on.

Sometimes it isn't difficult to like my dad the way he is. When I get him on the phone, for example, I feel that he's there for me. As if he was the happiest human being alive, happy about not being tied down and having nothing to lose but his freedom. But even then, I know that whenever he gets too tired of everything, he has no choice but to move on anyway.

When mom was in a good mood, she'd say, "Maybe he's just going in circles, and when he comes home next time, he'll stay."

I don't know whether she said it because she knew how much I hoped for it, or if she hoped for it too.

We were approaching Vicksburg. A few miles outside of town, Highway 61 moved closer to the river, and I could see the city in the distance, elevated on a low chain of hills. The armies of the South and the North fought over this town for weeks toward the end of the Civil War. The soil out there had soaked up the blood of thousands of soldiers. On the fields, where they had fallen, corn was growing.

We both starred out the window. I didn't know what JB was thinking, but I was thinking of history class and of Hanna, who didn't care about history one bit. I had meant to call her from Memphis and tell her I'd found JB and would soon return to Winstel.

"What are you thinking about?" JB asked when we left Vicksburg behind us.

I told him about Hanna. Not everything, of course. I told him about that day we learned about Vicksburg in history class and about Hanna writing me a letter on a small piece of paper instead of paying attention. And how she got caught and Mr. Blanchard, our English and history teacher, asked her to read the letter out loud. Hanna refused to do so, and when Mr. Blanchard wanted to take the piece of paper from her, she quickly stuffed it in her mouth and swallowed it. The whole class was watching and waiting for a reaction from Mr. Blanchard. However, he was nobody's fool and only said with biting mockery: "Bon appétit, Hanna! What's for dessert?"

The class burst into laughter, and Hanna turned bright red, wishing the ground would open up and swallow her. My friend Wayne threw a McDonald's ketchup packet to her, and Mildred Meigs pulled a can of Seven-Up from somewhere and gave that to her as well.

Later, when we sat by the Brewster Pond, watching the clouds and listening to the bullfrogs, I wondered what was in the letter. Hanna said it was a poem.

In those days, when she was about sixteen, Hanna wrote the craziest lyrics. Some of them I remember to this day, like this one:

> As wind in the grass the thoughts flow
> In one direction, away from me
> I stand there, feeling the blades of grass
> And don't know where I am
> Night envelops me
> Not just me
> I wanted to see
> What I cannot
> I long for the morning
> And to recognize you
> My beloved

I didn't know what this meant. Hanna had a whole collection of these poems hidden away somewhere in her parents' house, in a diary or something. I think I'm the only person she read any of them too.

We arrived in Leland at noon. Still, nearly three hours left until Memphis. JB was asleep, and I hoped he wouldn't start snoring. But it wasn't long before he did. One of the passengers sitting across from us looked up from his newspaper but didn't say anything. Only when the snoring got louder did he speak up.

"Kid, why don't you pinch Grandpa's nostrils? That's bound to help."

"He's asleep," I said.

"He's disturbing us," said the man.

"He isn't," said the woman sitting opposite him, with a child next to her. All three of them were black, but they weren't together. "Old people snore, that's the way it is. My husband never snored when he was young. And now he snores like a trooper."

"He's disturbing me," said the man, who wasn't interested in the woman's story. "I want to read in peace."

I woke JB. He looked around, confused because I had torn him from a deep sleep.

"You were snoring, Grandpa," I said.

He sat up and looked out of the window. "Where are we?"

"Beyond Leland."

"The next stop is Shaw," explained the woman. "We live in Shaw."

Nobody said anything.

The woman laughed. "I know, nobody lives in Shaw," she said. "Shaw is a dreary little place."

I could have said the same thing about Winstel, and under no circumstances did I want to spend the rest of my life there.

Now I'm still here, writing this book, without even knowing who is supposed ever to read it.

Sometimes, I think that nobody wants to read stories like this anymore. Nowadays, what people seem to want is a lot of shooting and car chasing. Action in every line of a story, otherwise they lose their patience. This book, perhaps, is a love story.

When we were traveling to Memphis on the Greyhound, I didn't know whether Crazy Legs was still alive. But he kept appearing in my thoughts, like a ghost who wouldn't leave you in peace. I don't believe in ghosts, but sometimes I thought Crazy Legs had it in for me because I brought JB and Lilly back together.

Only recently did I learn that Crazy Legs was dead. I got a letter from Sara Carter in Memphis. With a shaky hand, she wrote that some kids had found Crazy Legs in a dumpster in a New Orleans back alley. Somebody had smashed his skull in with a piece of two-by-four and stolen his shoes. He was barefoot and had seventeen cents in the pocket of his trench coat, which was full of holes, along with an empty Budweiser bottle and an old dance club ticket. Apart from that, he carried a piece of paper with my name on it and my address in Winstel. I figured he was the one who had sent me the newspaper clipping about JB's release from prison. Perhaps he wanted to get some burden off his chest. Something he'd been carrying around since the day JB got sentenced to life in prison. I couldn't figure out where he might have gotten my address, but it worried me.

The others are somehow around me, too, as I write this book. Sara Carter, the street sweeper on Beale Street, the cops in Hattiesburg, Mr. Ogden and his high-and-mighty son, Benedict, Pete "White Shoes" Bowles, the shoe shiner, the owner of the Thai restaurant, and all the others I met. And my father too, of course, who hasn't called in months and who still hasn't come to Winstel to drive to Memphis with me and spread Lilly's ashes over the Mississippi, as she had wished.

The trip to Memphis tired out JB; he hadn't traveled as far in fifty years. He had never left Hattiesburg, not even back when he was released.

At three o'clock in the afternoon, we finally arrived in Memphis.

Getting off the bus, JB almost stumbled. I managed to hold onto him. When I asked him if he wanted to sit down first at the bus station, where it was cool, he shook his head. However, he looked pretty tired. I was worried he would keel over just when we were about to arrive at Lilly's place, but he hung in there.

In the taxi, he suddenly seemed on edge.

"Maybe we should have called her first."

"We're almost there, Grandpa."

He remained silent until we arrived in front of the Harvest Moon. He stepped out of the taxi and looked at the two-story brick building with white window frames and doors. There was a large cobblestone plaza with four columns and stairs that led up to the door.

I paid the taxi driver, and he put our luggage on the first step. I carried the leather case with JB's old ham worth twenty thousand bucks as if there also would have been a dozen raw eggs in it. Now, I was a little nervous too. Suddenly, my mouth felt as if I had swallowed cotton. Until we arrived, I had imagined how it would be. We would walk up the stairs, enter the lobby, and got greeted by the myna bird. "Fancy caviar?"

And then we would wait for Lilly.

Finally, we were here.

We went up the stairs together and entered the lobby. The myna bird gave a shrill scream. "What do you want? An old hat to drum on?"

JB noticed some people watching us suspiciously, even

though we were too far from their table to steal their cake.

The lady at the reception desk recognized me, but her curiosity got drawn to JB.

"That's my grandfather," I said. "JB Swift."

"Good day, Mr. Swift," said the woman. "I believe Lilly is waiting for you."

JB didn't say anything. He sat down on one of the chairs and folded his hands in his lap. He looked old, confused, and insecure. It almost seemed as if he wanted to leave, to go back to Hattiesburg.

We had to wait a while, but then Rhonda turned up, a smile on her face. She held open the door, and in the half dark of the corridor, Lilly emerged, no more than a narrow silhouette at first, a vague glimmer, but then stepping into the light of the lobby. She was more beautiful than I'd ever seen her.

Rhonda offered her an arm, but Lilly didn't take it. She came toward us without hesitating. She moved swiftly, escaping the long shadows of a dream.

Her hands stretched out toward him, and his name was on her lips.

More than fifty years had gone by since they had last embraced. But not a second seemed to have gone by when JB took Lilly into his arms.

"You are here," she whispered. "You are here."

"I'm here," he said.

Nothing more they needed to say. At that moment I realized the miracle of true love is that it can make time stand still and last forever. They held each other as if they would never let go again. Then he spoke her name, and she spoke his.

And I saw it in her eyes the day she died. Just as happy as she had been when she had left Frank's Café at his side.

Neither time nor distance had been able to separate them. Not even death. I know, even though I cannot prove it, that wherever they are now, they are together.

CHAPTER 23
TEXAS BLUES

Lilly and JB clubbed their savings together and bought themselves a little house on Stratford Road, near Harrison Creek.

When JB died, Lilly sold it and moved back into the retirement home. I visited her as often as I could. And we wrote each other many letters. She told me all about JB and their love. About the house at Stratford Road, about the warm evenings on the little porch and about the melodies he created for her. She told me about the friends who came to visit, about the dog that got hit by a car when crossing the street, about the leaves from the trees dancing in the autumn wind, about an indoor plant she got to blossom, and about their long walks along the banks of the Mississippi.

Not once did they return to the place where disaster had hit them.

Beale Street was supposed to get a makeover, an entirely new face. That's what the city planners envisioned. They came and asked JB for advice, wanted him to tell them how it had been in the old days, about the people he had known, to lead them back through his memories to the Royal Blue, which they were planning to rebuild.

Lilly wrote me a letter when she read in the newspaper that Sara Carter had died. And then she wrote that JB had unexpectedly fallen ill.

I drove to Memphis straightaway.

He died three days after I got there. We were both

with him when he went. Uncle Lewis came too. And Lizette. My father wasn't there, and my mother had to work because she had started a new job. The day after his passing, JB got cremated. Lilly was given the urn with his ashes. After everyone had left again, we went to the Mississippi together to spread them. Just Lilly and me.

My father sent a card from Seattle.

"I'm with you," it read. "In my thoughts. Unfortunately, it's not possible any other way."

Later, I learned that he was in prison in Seattle at the time. Because of a brawl or something. In a bar. He had smashed in a pimp's teeth.

Now I'm waiting for him to drive to Memphis with me and the urn with Lilly's ashes. I know he'll turn up someday.

"No problem, Brad," he'll say with a grin. "Let's take Lilly back to Memphis."

Meanwhile, Rick has moved in with us. Most of the time, he lolls about in the armchair, sleeping with the TV on. When he isn't there, he hangs out downtown in the café, with the other old guys who all served in World War II, playing cards and drinking large quantities of coffee.

Rick is a small, wiry, bow-legged cowboy. He wears a hearing aid in one ear. He's deaf in the other and maintains that his eardrum exploded when he killed Miguel Santana, the infamous Border Bandit, in Del Rio, a small town on the Mexican border. This story is as old as Texas, and I don't believe anyone in Winstel buys it, but one day, when I've finished this book, I might write a book about Rick and the time he was a Texas Ranger and carried a dangerous weapon on his hip. Rick can tell stories until your ears fall off. And sometimes he hangs out on the playing field of the school, and the kids all sit around him captivated.

Rick has been with my mother for a few months. I don't know exactly how that came about. All of a sudden, he was there with his beat-up leather suitcase full of rags and his old saddle and all the gear he'd worn when he was a Texas Ranger, and later as a trick-shot artist and knife-thrower. He put the suitcase in the small storage room in the yard. And each time I leave the house through the back, I see the suitcase there with its massive lock, and I wish he would open it for once and show me the treasures I assume it holds.

Rick treats my mother well. She can scream at him, and he doesn't hear a thing, because, at times, he just switches off his hearing aid, if he wears it at all.

I like him, wrinkles and all. His deepest wrinkles are almost black because he rarely washes. But he doesn't smell bad for all that, and my mother washes his shirts for him so that he can put on a fresh shirt every day. Not the trousers. The trousers he wears for a week at a time, but he likes to put on a clean shirt every day.

I'm glad he is here with us. He's a man without relatives, has never been married, and has no kids. He last worked on the Brewster Ranch, but after the fall roundup, he came to Winstel and asked around for a place he could spend the winter. My mother heard about it and said there was a box room at the back of the house she could put in a bed. And so she did, and he's been with us ever since, hammering around the house, whenever there needed to be some hammering done. In the evenings, he occupies the armchair in front of the TV and watches the garbage my mother likes. Only when she's not around he searches for a different channel, and then he sits there watching Old Westerns until he falls asleep. I've seen him sleeping in the middle of Rio Bravo when Angie Dickinson throws the flower pot through the window, and Ricky Nelson jumps out of the hotel window, throws the rifle to John Wayne, and the shooting begins. Sometimes, I hunker down with him, and we watch these ancient flicks together, and I'm still watching after he long fell asleep; gunfighter movies with Randolph Scott or Audie Murphy, Gunfight at the O.K. Corral with Burt Lancaster and Kirk Douglas, or Tombstone with Henry Fonda.

People don't seem to watch Westerns anymore. To this day, Mitch gets the runs every time he hears shooting, though he would love to be a cowboy. I'm not joking. Something like that may be hard to explain in medical terms, but maybe it's not the banging and the shouting that frightens him, but the anger reaching deep down into his guts at the thought that he might miss something on another channel, like The Simpsons.

"How's your book coming along?" Rick sometimes asks me when we bump into each other.

"It's coming along fine," I'd answer.

"What?"

"Fine, I said!"

"Go write a Western, kid! There ain't no good Westerns anymore!"

As for Hanna, there is not much to be said. She studies at the Texas Christian College in Fort Worth. Even though that's not a long way from Winstel, I've never been there. She plays softball for the college team, and once in a while, she sends me a poem. I don't know what will become of our friendship. Her father told me she has a boyfriend who wants to make a career in politics. That's fine by me. She probably won't be able to forget, just as I'm unable to, what happened by the Brewster Pond.

Wayne is in San Antonio. He works for an advertising company.

My father called yesterday. Wanted to know what was going on.

"You know," I said. "Not much."

"You got to get out of there, son."

For an instant, I held my breath. He had never called me son before.

"You aim at going to college?" he asked.

"I guess that's what I do."

"Good for you. And your mother. Get out of that house. Start a new life. I always wanted to do that, start a new life, I guess, but I never had the guts to do it, Bradley. Not even when I met your mother."

I said nothing, just waited for more to come. My father had never talked to me that way. The hardships he had to endure had maybe softened him up, I thought, made him more human.

"You know, with me a new life gets old quick. But there is one thing you have to know, Bradley."

"What is it?" I almost called him dad.

He chuckled.

"It is hard, isn't it?"

"What?"

"To call me dad."

I didn't say anything. We both fell silent for a long time.

"Brad, I will always love you," he said suddenly. "Don't ever forget it. You and your mom."

I choked.

"I got to go now, Brad."

"Bye," I said. "Bye, dad."

The line was dead. I don't think he heard me saying it. He was in a hurry. I sat there by the phone for some time just thinking about him. Then I went outside, checking if the Rimrocks were still there. They still were. Nothing around me had changed. But my heart was aching.

How about Alesha? You know, I never heard from her again. Looking back, I think she never really existed in the first place, but she wasn't merely a dream, of course. What I mean is probably not easy to understand, but I believe I was perfectly happy, at the time, to imagine Alesha the way I wanted her to be, even though it didn't have much to do with who she was.

And sometimes, when I sit up there on that old water tower in the evening and watch the sun go down, and shadows crawl up the slopes of the Rimrocks, I pick up JB's guitar and play for her. And for Lilly.

CONTENTS

Books in German by ARAVAIPA:

Werner J. Egli:

Tunnel Kids	978-3-03864-010-3
Heul doch den Mond an	978-3-03864-008-0
Der erste Schuss	978-3-03864-004-2
Der letzte Kampf des Tigers	978-3-03864-000-4
Black Shark	978-3-03864-002-8
Aus den Augen, voll im Sinn	978-3-03864-003-5

Hubert Flattinger:

Baboon	978-3-03864-001-1
Sommersprossen auf dem Asphalt	978-3-03864-006-6

Werner Färber:

Willst du Stress	978-3-03864-005-9

Maja Gerber-Hess:

Das Jahr ohne Pit	978-03-03864-012-7

Joachim Friedrich:

Ana-Lauras Tango	978-03-03864-015-8

Now also in English!

Werner J. Egli

TUNNEL KIDS

ISBN 978-3-03864-408-8

„Composed in beautiful, sensual, and lyrical language, Tunnel Kids by Werner J. Egli is an engaging story of Santiago Molina, a fifteen-year-old boy who leaves his small village near San Cristobal de las Casas and travels to Mexico City to start a new life."
ROMAULD DZEMO, SF Book Review

„A gripping page-turner ..."
Londond (GB) Book Fair

„Books like Tunnel Kids are especially important right now as immigration to the United States is becoming more of a flashpoint in political discourse and politics. Stories like this remind us that most of the immigrants coming to the US are seeking safety and a better life, not a free ride.
HEIDI KOMLOFSKE-ROJEK,
publisher of the San Francisco Book Review